THE
SILVER COACH

C.S. ADLER lives with her husband and three sons in Niskayuna, New York, where she was a middle-school English teacher for several years. She has been a full-time writer since the publication of her first book, *The Magic of the Glits*, which won both the William Allen White Award and the Golden Kite Award. Since then, more than fifteen books for young readers have been published, including *Goodbye Pink Pig* and *Some Other Summer*, both in Avon Camelot editions, and *The Shell Lady's Daughter*, a 1983 Best Book for Young Adults. Several of Ms. Adler's books have been published in England, Denmark, Germany, and Japan.

THE
SILVER COACH

C.S. ADLER

AN AVON CAMELOT BOOK

AVON BOOKS
A division of
The Hearst Corporation
105 Madison Avenue
New York, New York 10016

First Avon Camelot Printing: November 1988

CAMELOT TRADEMARK REG. U.S. PAT. OFF. AND IN OTHER COUNTRIES, MARCA
REGISTRADA, HECHO EN U.S.A.

Printed in the U.S.A.

OPM   10 9 8 7 6 5 4 3 2 1

For our son, Steven,
who gave us the silver coach
and other joys

1

After the farms nestling in the green laps of the Vermont hills gave way to dark pine woods, Chris's mother said, "We're almost there."

Chris, sitting alone in the back of the car, looked out at the frowning woods and lost the little hope she had that the summer might turn out all right. Outside the droning safety of the car, dark trees locked into each other shutting out the late afternoon sun. Chris's little sister, Jackie, who was sitting up front snug against their mother, asked fearfully, "Grandma Wallace doesn't live in the woods, Mommy, does she?"

"Grandma Wallace likes the woods," their mother said. "She likes her privacy. She could have lived anywhere after your grandfather died. But what did she pick? A summer cottage they'd bought for their retirement."

Chris wondered if the disapproval in her mother's voice meant that she disliked Grandmother Wallace, or if it was just that this grandmother was Daddy's mother. Since the divorce started, Mother got angry about everything to do with Daddy. What was Grandmother Wallace like anyway? All Chris recalled from one visit five years ago, when she was seven and Jackie was two, was a trace of plump, soft fingers. Not enough to turn Grandmother Wallace from a stranger into someone familiar. Yet she was going to be in charge of Chris and Jackie for the whole summer, while their mother went to school for the special nursing courses she needed. Strangers always made Chris feel awkward and uncomfortable.

"I don't want to stay with Grandma Wallace all alone," Jackie whined. She turned her kitten face up toward her mother so that Chris could see the fear rounding her sister's bright eyes. "She looks mean."

"How do you know how she looks, Jackie?" Mother's tired face turned toward Jackie briefly before her eyes returned to the road. "First of all, you won't be alone, you'll have your big sister to take care of you; and second of all, Grandma Wallace is not mean. She's a perfectly nice woman."

"Chrissie showed me her picture. Her eyes are all squeezed together like a mean old witch."

"Chris! *Why* did you show Jackie that old photograph? Why did you have to do that?" The exasperation in her mother's voice needled Chris into defending herself.

"Jackie wanted to see what Grandmother Wallace looked like. I didn't see anything wrong in showing her the picture." Chris was always having to defend herself against her mother lately, ever since their father had left the house. It was bewildering, the way her mother acted now, as if she expected Chris to be an adult responsible for herself, for Jackie, and for everything in the house as well.

"It's a terrible picture. She was squinting into the sun," Mother said.

"It's the only picture we have of her," Chris said.

Then she probed cautiously, "Don't you like Grandmother Wallace, Mother? You never took us to see her before. We see our other grandmother a lot."

"Yes," Jackie threw in before their mother could answer. "Why couldn't we stay with Grandma Sissy instead?"

"Grandma Sissy's going to California to visit your aunt for the summer. I told you that. As for Grandma Wallace, the reason we never saw much of her . . . well, first of all, she and your grandfather lived all over the world. They were always so far away. Then they had a special person living with them, a person your father couldn't stand being around, so . . . so we never visited them much, and they . . . it was just not a close relationship, your father and his parents."

"Why wasn't it a close relationship?" Chris asked cautiously, wary of a sudden eruption of temper as she pushed toward the edges of her mother's patience.

"I told you. Your father couldn't stand his sister."

"His sister was the special person? Will she be there?"

"No, she's dead."

Everyone was dead, Chris thought, Grandfather, Daddy's sister. Only Grandma Wallace was left. That didn't sound very promising.

"I bet Daddy would have taken care of us if you'd let me ask him," Chris blurted out and immediately wished the words back in her mouth. Her mother jerked the car to a stop at the side of the road. Chris sucked her breath in. Twice in the past month her mother had slapped her for no reason. Chris drew her long, slender bones tightly together to make herself small, but this time Mother only looked at her hard.

Mother's face was very pale. All the tired lines were dug in deep, and the blond hair hung in limp spaghetti

3

strands around her neck. She said in a paper thin voice that cut Chris, "Your father's so great to you, isn't he? Just like he kept his promise on your birthday, didn't he? And I'm the mean one who won't let you stay home so you can go to those ballet lessons you want. Well, I'm sorry you've got such a rotten mother, but maybe I wouldn't be so rotten if I didn't get stuck with all the rotten jobs, like having to go out and support us all and then coming home to take care of a daughter who does nothing but complain and expect things I can't give her."

"I try to help!" Chris cried.

"Oh, sure you do! With that look on your face like everything's too much for you. You'd do anything to please your father, but doing anything for me is too much. I ask you to babysit for Jackie and you want to see your friends. I make you put down your book and vacuum the living room, and you act like I'm working you to death."

Why should I do anything for you, Chris thought. You hate me anyway. "No matter what I do for you, Mother, you always say it's not done right," she said, trying hard to keep her voice flat even, still afraid of the simmering temper.

"Mommy, don't be mad," Jackie said, touching her mother timidly, then cautiously patting her arm. Mother put her arms around Jackie and rested her chin on Jackie's silky, dark hair.

"Listen, I don't like having to leave you with your father's mother any more than you like being left there, but I don't have any choice. If I don't take this intensive course this summer, I won't make enough to cover the grocery bills this winter, and if you think your father is taking care of all our bills—he isn't." She swallowed

4

after she said this and looked upset. Then she released Jackie and started the car again. Chris let her muscles unknot and sagged.

They turned onto a narrow dirt road and began climbing. The woods that climbed with them squeezed out the sunlight. The house they saw when they finally broke into a clearing on top of the mountain was built of dark wood and had a steep, peaked roof. It looked lonely in the middle of the mowed grass, with the distant mountain tops a silent audience behind it.

"She won't eat us, will she?" Jackie whispered.

"She's not a witch! Would I leave you with her if she was a bad person?"

Jackie looked at her mother anxiously without answering, and Chris realized that even Jackie, who seemed securely wrapped in her parent's love, was not as trusting as usual. Their mother was acting so unpredictable, so unlike herself these days. She said it was because their father had left them and because of the divorce. Christ suspected it might be the other way around—that their father had left because Mother was so angry and yelled so much. After all, Daddy hadn't changed. He was still as kind and loving as ever, even if he hadn't come on her twelfth birthday.

"Oh girls!" their mother cried. "Stop looking at me like that. I'm not doing anything bad to you. Don't you know how much I love you? You're all I have now."

But then she led them right up to the dark, peaked house even though Jackie began to cry when she saw the stump with the ax head stuck into it.

"What are you wailing about?" Mother asked.

Jackie went on crying.

"What is she making such a fuss about? Chris, did you tell her something to frighten her?"

5

"Me? Why do you always blame everything on me?" Chris asked, the hurt stinging as much as a slap.

Mother put her arms around Jackie again. "Jackie, Jackie baby, don't cry. The summer will pass so quickly. Before you know it, we'll be going back home together again."

Jackie clung to her mother. "Don't leave us here, Mommy. Don't leave us," she whimpered. Chris stood watching them, feeling left out.

"I can't stand it," Mother said to the stone that served as the bottom step for the front door stoop. "I can't stand it anymore." She knocked on the door. It squeaked when it opened just like a witch's door. Terror stopped Jackie's tears. She stood there with her mouth open. Chris shivered too, remembering that it was going to be just Grandma Wallace and them, alone for a whole summer.

The sweet smell of baking cookies floated out the open door. A brown stump of a lady with a curiously smooth cap of white hair above a round face stood looking at them. Chris felt as if her grandmother's wide-apart gray eyes were seeing right into her. She dropped her own eyes quickly.

"Welcome!" Grandmother Wallace said. "You got here just in time to help me get the cookies out of the oven. Would you like some, girls?"

Chris looked up. She knew enough not to believe an adult who changed her tone to suit a child. But Grandmother Wallace had kept her voice tuned as if she were speaking to an adult.

"No cookies, thank you," Jackie said quickly. *Hansel and Gretel* had made a big impression on her; she was still frightened, Chris thought.

"Don't those cookies smell delicious!" Mother said

6

in a fake, cheerful way. Her glance warned her daughters to be polite.

"Come in," Grandmother Wallace said. "Unless you girls would rather roam around and stretch your legs— look the place over while your mother and I sit down to some coffee?"

Chris understood. Her grandmother wanted to talk in private with her mother. About what? About them? Or the divorce maybe. "Can we go wherever we want?" Chris asked.

"Sure can. Just don't get off in the woods out of sight of the house. We don't want to have to send a search party for you the first day."

"I want to go inside," Jackie said hastily. Their grandmother's joking about getting lost had probably alarmed her.

"Inside's fine. Just make yourselves to home. Why don't you see if you can guess where you're going to sleep."

Jackie took Chris's hand and let Chris lead her into the house. If no adults were around, Jackie often turned to her for help. Usually Chris liked that. If Jackie were not such a terrible show-off, she would be a pretty good sister.

The front door led right into a small kitchen. A stairway with a funny handrail made like a long, smooth, twisted bone ran upstairs along a wall of big stones which turned out to be the back of a chimney for the fireplace in the living room. The fireplace separated the kitchen and the living room, into which Chris led Jackie just as her mother agreed that a cup of coffee would be nice.

"Is she a witch?" Jackie whispered, making Chris bend way down so she could say it softly into her ear.

Chris considered. Then she let herself do one of the little meanies that were so hard to resist with Jackie. "She might be. We'll have to be careful."

"How?" Jackie asked.

"Just stick close to me and do like I tell you."

"Maybe we should go back to the car and hide."

"No. Mother would just find us and bring us back."

"Mommy doesn't know she's a witch, does she?"

Chris thought of the way adults were always making such a fuss about how cute Jackie was. "Maybe she does. Maybe she wants to get rid of us."

"No, she doesn't."

"How do you know?" But Chris was already ashamed of herself for taking the meanie so far. Not that Jackie ever seemed to notice. Jackie was so lucky. Everybody loved and petted her. The only person who really loved Chris was her father. "You're my best girl," he used to tell Chris when he lived at home, and she would make a snack for him or shine his shoes. He hated shining his own shoes. Why hadn't he taken her with him when he left? She loved him more than anybody. She was happy when she was with him.

"Look!" Jackie said. Her pudgy finger shook as she pointed at the enormous copper pot standing on the hearth next to the fireplace. The pot was large enough to cook a girl Jackie's size in.

"*Hansel and Gretel* is just a fairy tale. You know that," Chris said. And then to distract Jackie from the copper pot, she said, "Now look at that big table over by the windows. I wonder why she needs such a big table."

They walked past two armchairs and a couch to a table that ran the whole width of the room. The windows behind it framed a crowd of silent mountains stretching off to gray humps that might have been farther mountains, or just clouds.

"Maybe she has a lot of company," Jackie said.

"Mother said she likes to be alone." Chris wondered why her father didn't like his sister who had died. Mother had been hiding something about Daddy's sister. Their aunt, Chris thought. How strange to have both a grandmother and an aunt they didn't know.

"I don't like to be alone. I like to play with my friends," Jackie said babyishly.

"It doesn't look like we'll have anybody but each other to play with here," Chris said, regretting again the loss of her own two close friends and the ballet lessons she had so looked forward to.

"What will we do all day?" Jackie asked.

"I don't know. Something probably. Let's look upstairs."

Their grandmother and mother were too deep in conversation to notice them as they climbed the stairs that curved up around the back of the fireplace. Chris heard her mother say, "He's gotten so selfish. He doesn't care what he's doing to us. He says I have to learn to cope." It made Chris angry to hear her mother complaining about her father as if everything were his fault. Why didn't Mother admit it was all her screaming and nagging and crying that drove Daddy away! Why should he stay home when Mother was so awful to live with? He was a laughing man. He liked to play. He liked to enjoy life. All Mother wanted to do was save money and make the house look nice. It was boring to work all the time. And just because Chris was older, Mother expected her to work all the time too. She didn't expect Jackie to do anything. It wasn't fair.

Upstairs was all attic, an open space the size of the

house, windows looking down on the woods and a pond on one side. The pond had a small bridge over to an island big enough for one clump of trees. It looked like a lovely place to play, if only there were someone to play with. Chris thought of her friends. Now that she was gone for the summer, Amy and Seema would turn to each other. When she got back next fall, they would be best friends, and she would be outside. Amy had planned to take Miss Jason's summer ballet class with her. In school during every lunch period this past month, they had talked about whose mother would drive and about getting toeshoes and about practice exercises and —it wasn't fair.

"There's two beds," Jackie said, pointing.

Below one window two beds were made up with colorful red bedspreads.

"Is *that* where we're supposed to sleep?" Jackie asked.

"Maybe."

"I don't like it, Chris."

"Why not?"

"There's no walls."

Chris nodded. The room was too big, filled with dark spaces under the low part of the roof, boxes and tables with junk on them, shelves, and chairs without slats or with broken arms. The only proper bedroom part was where the beds were. Everywhere else was just lurking attic shadows where things might be hiding that could come out at night and steal up on you while you slept.

"Maybe there's a room for us downstairs," Chris said. She took Jackie's hand first this time as they went back down.

"He doesn't even want to see the girls any more," their mother was saying. "And he used to be so crazy about them—Jackie especially."

10

Liar! Chris thought. You know that isn't true! It was not Jackie but Chris whom Daddy was crazy about—*still was*. Chris walked right past her mother and grandmother, pretending she had not heard, pressing her lips together hard. She and Jackie looked into the bathroom down the short hall from the kitchen and then into a bedroom. Maybe, Chris thought, it was her mother who was the witch, poisoning Grandmother Wallace's mind against their father like that.

This bedroom was a proper one, with a bed, dresser, shelves with knickknacks and books, lilacs on the curtains at the window, and lilac-colored walls. On the wall beside the bed were framed photographs of all of them, Jackie and Chris in a swing pushed by their father, their parents' wedding picture, Grandpa Wallace, Jackie's baby picture, and Chris's school pictures. The room was obviously their grandmother's.

"See," Chris said. "Grandmother isn't a witch."

"Why not?"

"Because of the photographs. A witch wouldn't have photographs of her grandchildren on the wall, would she?"

"No?" Jackie looked puzzled, but willing to be convinced.

"I think we could eat some cookies."

"Okay, but . . ."

"But what?"

"If she's a regular grandma, how come she didn't kiss us hello when we came?"

Chris studied Jackie's pretty, round face. Jackie could be so smart sometimes. She herself had not even noticed that, but it *was* odd. Grandma Sissy was always kissing them. "Maybe she doesn't like to kiss people," Chris suggested.

11

"And why didn't we ever see her before?"

"Mother told us why," Chris said, growing impatient as Jackie built up her case and reinfected Chris with a creepy unease. A grandmother you never saw was strange. Even Seema saw her grandmother once a year, and Seema's grandmother lived in India, which was on the other side of the world.

"Look at this, isn't it pretty?" Chris asked Jackie, choosing from the knickknacks a red, lacquered box with flowers to distract her. Jackie nodded. She reached out to stroke a green rock carved like a funny-looking animal. It stood next to a painted, lace-edged fan in a silk-lined case that Chris thought was really beautiful. A graceful china lady wearing a tutu stood on one toe next to the fan.

"She looks just like you in your costume," Jackie said.

Chris smiled. Jackie could be so sweet. Chris carefully touched the stiff net skirt on the pink and white figurine. Sometimes, when she had her costume on and looked quickly over her shoulder into the mirror, she got a glimpse of herself being beautiful. But mostly she was too long and thin and pale. She felt beautiful when she danced though. Mrs. Jason said that if Chris was serious enough, she could become a real ballet dancer. But now, of course, Mrs. Jason wouldn't believe Chris was serious anymore. "The summer class is essential for serious students," Mrs. Jason had said.

"Look, Chris! The doors open and the wheels turn," Jackie said, holding up a coach made of silver lace. The coach was fairylike, as lovely as the dancer, more beautiful than the fan.

"You'd better not play with that. It might break," Chris said, sounding like her mother.

12

Jackie set the coach back on the shelf. Chris reached out one finger and touched it carefully. She felt a strange tingle and withdrew her finger. Then, curious, she again touched the fragile, intricately twisted silver wires that formed the coach. Once more she felt that tingle, as if the coach were emitting a tiny electric current. Weird, Chris thought, and she asked her sister, "Did you feel anything funny when you picked up the coach?"

Jackie shook her head negatively, no longer interested in the coach. "I wish Mommy would take us home with her. Even if Grandma isn't a witch, I don't want to stay here."

Chris touched the coach again experimentally. Nothing now. She had been imagining things. The coach was just a pretty ornament. She sighed. "Maybe we won't have to stay here for long," she said.

"Why not?"

"I'm going to write a letter to Daddy tonight and ask him to come get us." The idea had just occurred to her. With their mother gone, who was to stop Daddy from taking them away with him? All Chris had to do was find a way to mail the letter without Grandmother's knowing. She wondered if the mailman came all the way up that long empty road through the woods to here. Thinking about it, she regretted just a little the impulse that had made her tell Jackie and include her in the plan of escape. If she had been smarter, Chris could have had her father all to herself. But it was too late now. She had said "us."

2

In the kitchen, when the time came to kiss goodbye, Jackie burst into tears and clung to her mother's waist.

"You're going to have a wonderful summer here with your grandma," Mother said, sounding full of tears herself. "Be good, both of you. Jackie, please stop crying. You're making Mommy feel so bad. Chris, take care of her, will you? And write to me, okay?" She gave Chris a second peck on the cheek and kissed Grandmother Wallace, then disentangled herself from Jackie and ran. Jackie burst into tears and started after her mother.

"Jackie, come here now. I have something to show you," Grandmother Wallace said.

"Mommy!" Jackie wailed.

"She's such a baby," Chris said, fighting off her own panicky tears by criticizing Jackie.

"Would you go catch her and bring her back for me, Chris?" Grandmother asked.

Chris nodded, reassured by the steady look in her grandmother's clear, gray eyes and certain nobody with such round, downy cheeks could be mean. She ran down the steps, caught Jackie and lugged her back, half carrying, half dragging her. "Grandmother wants to show us something," she said. "Stop acting like a baby now, Jackie."

Jackie gave a cry of despair. Chris looked around and saw the disappearing rear end of their car. They were stranded now, alone in the dark woods with a stranger. Her confidence turned leaden and seemed to fall into her stomach. "It's going to be all right, Jackie," she said to reassure them both.

What their grandmother had wanted to show them was a book on the plants and animals of Vermont. "I wonder how many different specimens you could find just around that pond out there," Grandmother said as she pointed out the colored illustration of the life cycle of a frog, from egg through tadpole to green, bug-eyed adult.

"I don't like frogs," Jackie said.

"What kind of animals do you like?" Grandmother asked, sounding interested.

"Furry kinds like dogs and cats and rabbits."

"She likes the petting zoo," Christ said. "Whenever the petting zoo comes to the mall, Mother can hardly get Jackie away from it."

"I like kangaroos," Jackie said.

"And baby lambs," Chris said. Actually, she liked them too.

"Well," Grandmother said. "We have a lot of chipmunks and squirrels—they're furry—and maybe some rabbits. But they're all wild animals. You'd have to be very, very patient before they'd let you get close enough to touch them."

"How long till we can go home, Grandma?" Jackie asked.

15

"Don't be rude, Jackie," Chris said, an echo of her mother.

"Maybe after a while you'll enjoy staying here," Grandmother said. "I'll tell you a secret, Jackie. I was tickled pink when your mother asked me to take you girls for the summer. I've always wanted a chance to get to know my granddaughters. Now we'll have time to get acquainted."

"But I don't like frogs," Jackie said, her kitten face cross with tiredness.

"A nap before dinner would be nice, wouldn't it?" Grandmother said. "Did you find your beds upstairs?"

"Yes," Chris said, "but Jackie doesn't like it up there. She says there's too much room."

"Not cozy enough, huh? Well, we can fix that. We can build some partitions and make a real walled-off bedroom."

"How?"

"Oh, with wood and nails and boxes or panels or screens—however you like. We'll make a nice working project out of it together. Doesn't that sound like fun?"

Chris nodded. It did sound sort of interesting.

"We'll save it for a rainy day when we have to be in the house anyway," Grandmother said. "Do you think you can manage to sleep up there a few nights until we're ready to build, Jackie?"

"If Chrissie is with me," Jackie said.

Instead of helping get dinner, Chris stayed in Grandmother's bedroom until Jackie fell asleep. For the nap, Grandmother had given them a woolen afghan of gray and rose stripes that she had knitted herself. Chris lay quietly, examining her feelings for a minute after Jackie fell asleep. So far, she decided, this grandmother seemed all right, and it would be a relief not to have her mother

16

pecking at her all the time, for a while anyway. A pot
clanked in the kitchen. Carefully, to avoid waking Jackie,
Chris slipped out of the room and headed for the kitchen,
the only lighted space in the now dark house. Grandmother was peeling vegetables.

"I can set the table if you tell me where the dishes
are," Chris offered.

"Are you always such a good girl, Chris?"

"I try to be," Chris said.

"You must be a great comfort to your mother."

Chris didn't know what to answer. "Are the glasses
in this cabinet?" she asked, ignoring her grandmother's
remark.

That night Jackie set her pink toothbrush with the
Yogi Bear bottom opposite Grandmother's blue toothbrush in the bathroom holder. Then she amazed Chris
by going straight to Grandmother and kissing her cheek.
"Goodnight, Grandma," Jackie said, quite as if she had
never questioned why their grandmother had not kissed
them hello or wondered whether she might possibly be a
witch. Chris never understood how Jackie could adjust
to a situation so quickly.

Chris planted a kiss on Grandmother's other cheek
and wished her a second goodnight. Then she climbed
the stairs to the attic hand in hand with Jackie. They
were going to bed at the same time because, when Jackie
had balked at going upstairs alone, Grandmother had
said, "Well, Jackie, you took a long nap, so I guess you
can stay up late tonight."

Chris had been ready to object to being forced into an
early bedtime just because Jackie needed company. She
hoped she was not going to have to fight the battle of
separate bedtimes all over again here. It was unfair to
make a twelve-year old go to bed when a seven-year-old

did. Her grandmother seemed to read her mind. She said to Chris, ''It's just tonight because Jackie is in unfamiliar surroundings. We don't want her to be scared, do we?''

Soon after they were in bed, the light in the kitchen went off. Without the glowing stairwell lit by the overflow of light from the kitchen, the attic became all dark, moving shadows. The carbon-paper sky outside was poked through with stars, but over the drumming of the night insects came the sound of wind tossing tree branches madly about. The wind slid into the attic through spaces around the windows and made things rustle and creak. Jackie whimpered in her sleep. She always fell asleep so fast, while Chris had to lie struggling with the backwash of feelings the day had left her before she could let go. Chris shut her eyes, telling herself it was only the wind. Nothing was out there but wind and trees and small, furry animals. Nothing was in the attic but boxes. And what was in the boxes? Nothing . . . nothing . . . nothing but books and old things, probably. She reached across and touched Jackie's warm body. Then sleep snapped her up.

Later, Chris woke up suddenly when something leaped on her. Jackie, she realized. ''What's wrong?''

''I'm scared, Chrissie. I want to go home.''

''What are you scared of?''

''The noises.''

''Oh, don't be silly. It's only the wind. Do you want to sleep with me?''

''Let's go downstairs to Grandma's room. I don't like it up here.''

''What a little pest you are,'' Chris groaned.

''Please!''

''Oh, all right. Can you find your slippers?''

"I don't need them. Let's go." Jackie's hand was icy. She was shivering with cold or fear or both. They crept downstairs. The kitchen looked strange in the dark, the white refrigerator a hulking, headless ghost. They skittered down the hall. Chris inched open the door to their grandmother's room. Moonlight lit the mounded figure on the bed. Jackie whimpered. The mounds straightened into a dumpy, white-haired grandmother who got up at once and padded toward them.

"What's the matter?" Grandmother asked. "Scared of the noises?" She stooped and took Jackie into her arms and began rocking her gently.

"She was afraid so she woke up," Chris said and added bluntly, "and she thinks you might be a witch."

"A witch? Well, I've been called that before. Your father used to call me that when he got mad at me for something." Grandmother studied Chris with her piercing eyes. Then she said, "Come here, Chris. I have two arms for hugging, one for each of my granddaughters."

As if that was what she had been waiting for, Chris plunked down on the shag rug beside Grandmother and let herself be enfolded against the cushiony side. Usually Chris was not much for being hugged, unless it was by her father, but Grandmother was a comfortable hugger. Her skin smelled like rose petals, or maybe it was lilac, anyway some kind of flower, and the anger that had lumped in Chris dissolved a little.

"A cup of hot chocolate would be good before we go back to sleep, wouldn't it?" Grandmother asked.

"Yes," Jackie said. Chris got the cups out, pleased to have remembered where they were kept. They each ate a piece of the bread Grandmother had baked that morning.

"It has little chewy bits in it that are good," Chris commented.

19

"Oatmeal," Grandmother said. "I like to bake bread. It's fun to knead the soft dough. Did you ever do it?"

"No."

"We could try that some time, if you like. Tomorrow though, I'll show you where the blackberry bushes are. If you and Jackie help me pick, we can get enough to make some preserves. Blackberry preserves on fresh bread are delicious."

"How do you make preserves?" Chris asked.

"I'll show you tomorrow. You might want to make some to bring as presents for your parents and friends."

"Jackie can make some for Mother," Chris said. "I'll make my father his."

"You're a daddy's girl?" Grandmother asked.

"I hate my mother," Chris heard herself say. She caught her breath at what she had exposed. The eyes that saw too much studied her. Chris squirmed and thought, "she made me say it; she made me tell her that and it's not true anyway, leastways not all the time."

"Maybe it's a good thing if you all get a vacation from each other this summer," Grandmother said.

Chris was surprised that Jackie did not complain when Grandmother sent them back up to bed. The noises were still around, but Jackie fell asleep as if she no longer heard them.

For a long time Chris listened to the night sounds over the steady burr of the insects. All the whispers and creaks sounded harmless now, but Chris felt a hollow inside herself. It was no wonder everybody loved Jackie and nobody cared about her. She was not a nice person. Only nasty people hated their parents. She thought of her mother saying Jackie was Daddy's favorite. Her mother didn't know anything, but she wasn't hateful, not all the time, anyway.

Tomorrow Chris would write to her father. Maybe his answer would be that he could not take care of a little child like Jackie, but he would love to have Chris because she would be such a help to him. Jackie wouldn't mind staying here alone for a while. She never stayed unhappy for long, no matter what happened. First though, it would be good to learn how to bake bread. Chris imagined offering her father some home-baked bread and blackberry preserves as he sat at a kitchen table. "I made this just for you, Daddy."

"You're my best girl, Chris," he would say then as he had said before, before this year when he moved out and began forgetting to come see them when he had promised.

3

Yesterday's fears evaporated along with the morning dew. By the time Chris had helped Grandmother locate enough buckets for all three of them to go berry picking, Jackie was back to her normal, exuberant self. She was balancing on a low branch of a tree at the edge of the lawn when they came out of the garage.

"Look at me! Look at me!" Jackie squealed. "I climbed this tree all by myself."

"That's good, Jackie," Grandmother said. "It's a good climbing tree, but come along now. We're ready to go berry picking."

"I can climb higher even. I can climb right up to the top of this tree," Jackie boasted.

"Please don't try that," Grandmother said. "What would I do if you fell and hurt yourself? Come on down—*now* Jackie!" This last was said firmly, Chris was glad to hear. Jackie sat down on the tree branch and kicked her legs with her usual unconcern about doing as she was told.

"I can lie down on this tree and hang my legs and my

22

arms down," Jackie said, and proceeded to lie stomach down on the branch to show them. "See?"

"It'll be too hot to go berry picking if we don't get started right away," Grandmother warned.

"She's such a show-off," Chris said. "I'll get her, Grandmother." Chris ran across the yard to the tree, but, with a giggle, Jackie swung herself off and ducked past Chris.

"Grandma, Grandma! Watch me fly!" Jackie yelled as she wheeled around the yard with arms flung out, skimming the grass like a dragonfly. Chris almost caught up with her once, but Jackie veered in another direction just in time, laughing, and Chris tripped over a tree root and went sprawling.

"Did you hurt yourself, Chris?" Grandmother said.

"No, I'm all right." Chris stood up and brushed herself off. All she had hurt was her dignity.

"She has a lot of energy, doesn't she?" Grandmother said.

"Jackie's such a show-off. Sometimes other kids just won't play with her, she gets them so mad, but adults always think she's cute," Chris said irritably.

"Do *you* think she's cute?" Grandmother asked. Her level gray eyes were reading Chris's face as she answered.

"Sometimes she is," Chris said. "Sometimes I think she's an awful pest." Chris sniffed in disgust with herself. Here she was at it again—being mean, calling Jackie a pest. Why couldn't she at least keep her mouth shut? To make amends she added, "But Jackie is a sweet kid, basically. Like she never says mean things about anybody even if they're not nice to her, and she thinks everybody's nice."

"And you?" Grandmother asked. "Aren't you sweet, Chris?"

"No. I'm not. I wish I were. Mother says by biggest fault is that I'm too critical of people."

"I suspect there could be a connection between being critical of people and not being sweet. On the other hand, I don't think much of sweetness as a virtue, do you? Other virtues are so much more important."

"Like what?"

"Oh, like being honest, which you are—and making intelligent judgments, which you do—and being helpful, which you try to be."

"Thank you," Chris said. "It's nice of you to say that."

"I say just what I mean—like you." She smiled at Chris, and Chris smiled back, feeling good.

Jackie pranced up. "For you, Grandma." She offered a fistful of delicate blue flowers.

"Why, I never noticed we had bluebells in the yard, Jackie! That's what comes of sitting on a tractor to do my mowing. Thank you kindly, sweetheart. I'm partial to bluebells."

Grandmother was so delighted! Chris felt betrayed when, just as if she were not in a hurry now, Grandmother said she would just pop the flowers into a jar of water in the kitchen and be back in a minute. For a handful of wildflowers Jackie got called "sweetheart," a handful of wildflowers to win Grandmother over when Jackie had been acting so silly and making them wait. Maybe Grandmother didn't put a high value on sweetness, but she enjoyed it just the same.

"Jackie," Chris said. "You're such a little phony. What are you giving Grandmother flowers for? Has she got you under her spell?"

"What spell?" Jackie asked innocently. Yesterday's fears were too far away for her to even remember them.

"Chrissie, I like it here. We're gonna have fun this summer." Jackie reached for Chris's hand, but Chris shook her off.

"You are, maybe. I'm going to write Daddy to come get me. Have you changed your mind about coming too?"

"Coming where?" Grandmother asked, walking up behind Chris silently on the soft-soled moccasins, the kind Indians wore in the woods, she had told Chris at breakfast.

"What?" Chris asked to stall for time.

"Were you talking about your father?" Grandmother asked. "I got a letter from him a few days ago. He wrote that he might stop by here to see me on his way to New Hampshire."

"Soon?" Chris asked hopefully.

"Yes, I think so. I'll write and tell him you girls are with me. Then maybe he can plan to make a longer stopover."

"I might go with him when he leaves," Chris offered.

"Oh? That's disappointing. I've been looking forward to getting to know you this summer. But, of course, I understand how you might rather be with your father than an old party like me."

"I'd rather be with you," Jackie chimed. She linked her arm with Grandmother's and stood tiptoe to kiss her cheek. "You're just my size."

Grandmother laughed and hugged Jackie. Chris tossed her hair. Jackie was incredible. There was no sense in even trying to compete with a sister who oozed charm the way Jackie did.

The blackberry bushes were tangled nets of thorny brown branches speckled with green leaves and sweet, soft berries long as a thumb joint. Chris picked and picked until her fingers were purple with juice. Not a thought was in her head, just a concentration of black-berries. When she looked up, she saw that the bucket was half full. Grandmother's bucket was even fuller. Jackie's bucket was almost empty.

"Jackie hasn't saved any berries for the preserves," Chris noted. "She eats them all."

"I do not!"

Jackie's berry-smeared face made her indignant denial so funny that Chris and Grandmother both began laughing at her.

"I did *too* pick my share," Jackie insisted.

"Well, where are they then?"

"In your bucket, Chrissie. I put all I picked in your bucket."

"You did not! I picked this whole humongous bucketful by myself." Chris was annoyed at Jackie for trying to grab credit for even this small accomplishment. Her teachers were always telling her mother that Chris was a conscientious student. That meant she stuck with a job until it was done right, and she knew it was one of her good points. Jackie never stuck with anything.

"She might have put a few berries in when you weren't looking," Grandmother said mildly, as Chris frowned at her sister.

Chris ducked her head. There was no use arguing. Jackie never saw any truth that wasn't to her own advantage. She would swear to anything to make herself come out in the right. Chris turned back to picking berries, working in silence, not enjoying it any more. Jackie was quietly putting berries in Chris's bucket and getting some leaves mixed in.

"Stop that. You're ruining my berries," Chris muttered at her. Tears blurred her eyes. She hated berry picking. She hated her grandmother. She hated herself, and she didn't much like Jackie either.

The bucket was so heavy that Chris had a hard time hauling it back, but she would not complain. Then Grandmother saw her difficulty and said, "I'll take your bucket, Chris. It's easier for me to balance two."

"No, I can manage, thank you."

"Really, two makes it easier for me," Grandmother said.

Chris let her take the bucket then. She walked beside Grandmother thinking that, old as she looked, she must be pretty strong. Jackie was off chasing a yellow butterfly with black spots. "That's a swallowtail butterfly," Grandmother said to Chris. "Your father had a butterfly collection for a while as a young boy."

"Did he catch them?"

"Some. But mostly he bought already-mounted specimens. It was easier that way. He never had a lot of patience for hobbies, never seemed to stick with any for very long."

"Mother said you traveled all over the world," Chris said.

"Over a good part of it."

"But you came to live here."

"Yes. Does that seem strange to you, Chris?"

Chris looked at the pointy brown house standing alone in its field, surrounded by woods on three sides and mountains on the fourth. Why was this her grandmother's favorite spot? There were no stores or people or playgrounds or backyard pools for excitement, nothing but quiet.

"It's pretty here," Chris said. "But it's lonely."

"I don't mind being alone. In fact, I like it."

"And you don't ever miss being with people?"

"Sometimes, but then it's easy for me to go visiting."

"How? By airplane?"

"No. I have a magic coach that takes me."

Chris was startled. "Oh, Grandmother!" she said.

"Really I do. I'll show it to you this afternoon after we make the preserves."

"You're teasing me," Chris complained.

"No, I'm not. In fact, if there's someplace you'd really like to go, you may borrow my coach—if you can figure out how to use it."

"A magic coach," Chris repeated unbelievingly. "Grandmother, you're not serious." But even as she doubted, Chris remembered the silver coach and the curious tingle she had felt when she first touched it. "That little silver coach you have . . ." Chris began.

"Oh, you've noticed it already," Grandmother said. The wide-apart eyes looked at Chris very seriously under the white cap of hair. Chris felt a little tickle of excitement, but no fear. Surely this was the most mysterious of grandmothers, Chris thought, with her magic coaches and a strange daughter and liking to live all alone. Maybe Grandmother Wallace did have some witch blood in her somewhere.

4

The blackberry preserve manufacturing operation got delayed because Grandmother was out of paraffin. Paraffin was the wax that sealed off the jars of preserves with a whitish layer on top to keep bacteria from getting at the preserves and spoiling them.

"We'll have to drive down to Mabel's store. I want to introduce you to her anyway," Grandmother said.

"Who's Mabel?" Jackie asked.

"Mabel's my best friend."

Chris was curious to see what kind of a best friend her grandmother would have. The trip was even more interesting when she found out they were to go in the pickup truck, a new experience for both girls. The open deck behind the cab of the truck looked like fun.

"Why can't I ride in back?" Jackie mewed.

"Because you'd bounce right out going down this awful, bumpy road," Grandmother said. Jackie pouted and whined and pleaded, but Grandmother wouldn't give in. Chris was impressed. Jackie could make most adults give in, if not by charm, then by persistence.

"How far is Mabel's store?" Chris asked.

"About five miles."

"Does the mailman come up to your house?" Chris was thinking about the letter to her father. Even if he were already planning to come, he would be more likely to take her with him when he left if she asked him about it beforehand.

"The mailman leaves my mail at the store. Mabel is the postmistress as well as the storekeeper and the gas station attendant. She's also a wonderful companion. Sometimes when I'm out of sorts, she comes up to stay with me."

"Then who runs everything?" Jackie asked, finally settled in on the front seat between Chris and Grandmother.

"Her husband. You'll like Mabel. She's the way a child is supposed to be—always tells you the exact truth and never hides what she's thinking."

"Why do you say, 'supposed to be'?" Chris asked.

"Because children hide what they think just the way adults do. Don't they, Chris?"

Chris didn't answer. She was afraid she had already let Grandmother in on her private thoughts too much, and she didn't know what Grandmother thought about her or Jackie or anything that really mattered.

"What do you get 'out of sorts' from?" Jackie asked.

"Too much of my own company, I guess," Grandmother said cheerfully. They bounced all over the rocks on the dirt road. Chris was glad they were not standing in the open back.

"I'm a terrible driver," Grandmother said. "It's because I'm too short to see over the dashboard very well, even with this extra cushion I use."

"There's blocks of wood on the pedals so your feet can reach them," Jackie said.

"That's smart of you to notice," Grandmother said.

"Jackie's very smart. She always gets straight E's," Chris said, glad to be saying something complimentary.

"What are E's?"

"For excellent. I don't get all E's, but then it gets harder as you get older. Middle school is really hard, especially math. I hate math."

"I did too," Grandmother said. "Do you copy your friends' homework?"

Chris considered. Was it a trick question? She told a cautious truth. "Sometimes."

"I used to, too, sometimes. I was afraid if I didn't, I'd get left back," Grandmother said.

Chris was surprised a grandmother would admit such a thing and wondered if she would duck and hide if Chris asked her a personal question.

"You know," Chris said, "Mother said we never saw you much because Daddy didn't like his sister. Is that true?"

"Partly, yes. Partly it was other kinds of distances," Grandmother said, thinking about it. "Do you know about your Aunt Rise, his sister?"

"No."

"She died right after your grandfather died. It was a very unlucky year for me. She was three years younger than your father, and her brain was damaged when she was born so that she didn't grow mentally as she should have. But she was a dear person, very loving and gentle. Only your father didn't like her."

"Why not?"

"He had no patience with her slowness. She couldn't do the easiest things at all well—put on her clothes right or cut her meat at the table. She couldn't remember simple instructions for more than a minute. Then we

31

sent your father away to school and kept Rise home with us. That was for his own good, so he would get the education he needed. We were living in a very bad place for schools then. But I suspect he always imagined we kept Rise because we loved her better.''

"Did you love her better?" Chris asked.

Grandmother was silent for a minute, and Chris didn't think she was going to answer, but then she said, "Maybe we did love her more, in a way.''

She is honest, Chris thought, and didn't find her grandmother quite so strange any more.

The store was a square box on the main road with two gas pumps in front of it. Lots of shelves lined the wall over a couple of freezer chests and coolers. In one corner was a tick-tack-toe of mailboxes that opened only with the owners' keys.

"Look what I've got, Mabel!" Grandmother called to her friend. "This is Chris, and this is Jackie—my very own granddaughters."

"Well, look at you! Aren't they something!" Mabel said. "Never believe such pretty little things could come off a stumpy, old tree like you.''

"Grandma's not an old tree," Jackie protested fiercely.

Mabel and Grandmother laughed. Mabel was as skinny as Grandmother was plump and as tall as Grandmother was short. She had orange hair and wore long earrings and a fancy dress, as if she were going out to dinner. She looks weird, Chris thought.

"Your grandma is one game dame," Mabel told Jackie. "She's the salt of the earth, if you know what I mean."

Neither Jackie nor Chris did, but it was plain that Mabel admired their grandmother.

"Where am I going to pick up some plywood?"

Grandmother asked Mabel. "Have to section off a bed-room up there in the attic for the girls."

"I can have Charley pick some up for you when he goes through town tomorrow. Just tell me what you need."

"Grandmother," Chris said, "you don't need to spend money to build a room just for us for the summer." She considered quickly. "We could make it like a tent with sheets if we just tied some strings around to hang them from."

"Really? Would that be enough like a real room for you, Jackie?"

"I'm not going to be scared any more," Jackie said. "But I do like tents."

"Aren't you the smart little girl!" Mabel said to Chris.

"A tent sounds like a fine idea, Chris. I have all kinds of curtains and bedspreads and things we could use." Grandmother smiled at Chris and Chris felt proud of herself. It was nice to be the thoughtful, smart one for a change.

"How about visiting us soon, Mabel?" Grandmother said. "You could show the girls how to catch fish in the pond. You're the one who knows how best."

"I was thinking of paying you a visit anyway, Eve. Tell you what, let's make it next Monday. I know Charley's going to be around then to take over for me."

Mabel insisted that the girls take some candy. "Have some on me," she said, meaning it was her treat. The candy sticks in the open jars on the counter looked dusty to Chris, but she and Jackie took a couple of sticks each and thanked Mabel politely. Jackie sucked on hers on the way home. Chris thought she would try washing hers off first.

"Mabel is a real superwoman," Grandmother said as

she drove back up to the house. "She's had a difficult life, lost two sons, had a daughter with a real hard-luck marriage, and her husband sits around most of the time claiming he's too sick to work, letting her do his work and hers too. But Mabel keeps smiling. I think she gets more out of life than most people."

"She looks funny," Jackie said, expressing Chris's thought exactly.

"Well, so do I," Grandmother said. "We can't all be young and pretty like you."

"No," Jackie said. "I suppose not."

Grandmother winked at Chris. Chris smiled back. Maybe it was going to be a good summer after all. At least it would be interesting to get to know Grandmother Wallace until Daddy came to take Chris away with him. There was the tent to be built in the attic, and there was the silver coach. Chris wondered if the coach really was magic, though, of course, she knew it couldn't be.

5

Making blackberry preserves turned out to be easy. First they washed the berries and drained them, picking out the bits of leaves and sticks. Then they added the sugar and let the berries sit for a few hours before setting them on the stove to boil into a sweet syrup that would thicken into solid preserves when it cooled in the sterilized jars and was covered by a seal of paraffin.

"That was cinchy," Jackie said. "You know a lot of good stuff, don't you Grandma?" That made Grandmother hug her.

"It smells so good cooking," Chris said.

"Sometimes," Grandmother said, "I cook things just to enjoy the smell of them."

"Grandmother," Chris said. "You were going to show me the magic coach."

"So I was. Well, we'll just clean up the mess we made here, have a bite of lunch first, and then I'll show you my keepsakes."

"What's a keepsake?" Jackie asked.

"It's a thing you keep for the sake of remembering a time or a person you love," Grandmother said.

"I have a keepsake," Chris said.

"What is it?" Jackie asked.

"The rose that Daddy gave me after my first dance recital. I pressed it in my scrapbook."

"That must have been a very special occasion for you," Grandmother said.

"It was. I had a green tutu. It was spring. And Daddy gave me the flower. That made it really special. He knows how to make everything special."

"He doesn't all the time," Jackie said. "He forgot it was my birthday, and on *your* birthday, he didn't take you to the amusement park like he promised."

"He couldn't help that, Jackie," Chris said.

"Why couldn't he help it?"

"He said—don't you remember?—he said . . ."

"What?" Jackie asked.

"Oh, never mind. You're too young to understand anyway."

"You always say I'm too young," Jackie said. She pouted.

"Well, you *are* too young. You don't understand about the divorce or anything. It's because of the divorce that now Daddy doesn't come sometimes when he promises. He can't help it. Mother's always yelling at him and making him feel bad when he comes. And then when he does take us for a drive to visit some people, *you* have to get sick and throw up all over the car."

"I didn't do it on purpose!" Jackie's instant tears exasperated Chris. She turned her back on her sister and found herself pinched by feelings—anger at herself for being so mean again, anger at Jackie for criticizing their

36

father, and anger at Grandmother for comforting Jackie as she now was doing.

"Of course you didn't do it on purpose," Grandmother told Jackie. "And anyway, there's no sense fussing over things that are done and gone."

Chris felt scratchy inside, but she tried not to show it. She said, "I don't really feel like eating lunch. Couldn't we look at your keepsakes first?"

"Why not?" Grandmother said. "We don't have a schedule to keep to."

They finished cleaning up and followed Grandmother into her bedroom. First she showed them the Spanish fan which she said her husband had given her one summer in the South of Spain when she was pregnant with their father and went around feeling as if she were going to suffocate from the heat and the weight of the baby.

"I used to sit there playing with the fan and imagining I was an elegant lady instead of the tub of lard I looked like." She showed them how the flowered, gold-encrusted fan flicked open and closed with a touch, and how you were supposed to hold it to flirt with the boys with just your eyes showing. She made them both laugh when she held the fan over her stubby nose and blinked her eyes rapidly, showing them how to flirt.

"Let me try," Jackie begged, but Grandmother handed Chris the fan first.

Watching herself in the mirror, Chris thought she flicked the fan well and liked the way her eyes teased above it.

"You're naturally graceful," Grandmother said.

But Jackie went crazy over the fan. She invented a whole dance to go with it, getting wilder and wilder as she spun around until Grandmother begged her to stop before she broke something. With the fan back in its case, Grandmother went on to tell them about the wooden bear from Russia and the enamelled box. The carved, green jade god was a gift to celebrate the birth of her daughter, Rise, who was born when their father was three.

"We knew soon after she was born that she would always need us, all her life. She was so beautiful and helpless, and there was your father, just as strong and independent as he could be."

"Was Daddy a good little boy?" Jackie asked.

"Oh no! He was a real mischief, always off somewhere getting into trouble." Grandmother grinned with some mischief in her own eyes. "He liked to show off like someone else we know."

"Who?" Jackie asked innocently.

"Is that why you loved Rise more?" Chris asked, backtracking in the conversation.

"I don't know if I really loved Rise better," Grandmother said. "Just that she needed us so much more."

"Did Daddy travel to all the places where you got these things?" Chris asked.

"Only when he was little. We lived in Spain and then in England, where I got this ballerina, who looks a lot like you, Chris. Then we went to Morocco, and the town where we were to live there was not healthy for children. So we put your father in boarding school in England when he was only seven—Jackie's age, or a little older. That was a terrible decision for me to make, but it seemed the best thing for him. So I did it. That was when your grandfather gave me the silver coach."

She picked up the lacy coach they had touched the day before and put it in Chris's hand. Once again Chris felt the odd, tingling sensation.

38

"Your grandfather wanted to console me because I felt bad when your father went away. So he told me that the coach was magic. Whenever I missed my son, all I had to do was make a wish, and the coach would carry me to where he was."

"Magic!" Jackie whispered in awe.

"He was just trying to make you feel better, wasn't he?" Chris asked.

"That's what I thought," Grandmother said. "But one day I got an awful case of the blues, and I tried the coach. I can't tell you how, but it worked. Ever since then I've been able to make it work for me whenever I want to go to someone I love or revisit someplace that I'm homesick for. That's why I don't mind living up in the woods by myself, not as long as I can get away whenever I feel like it."

"But how do you make it work?" Chris wondered.

"You have to find *that* out for yourself."

Chris fingered the coach, thinking not about it, but about her father as a little boy. She had never thought of her father as a child before. "Did Daddy always go to boarding school?" Chris asked.

"Most always, except on long vacations when he came home to us. Then, when he grew up, he went away to college in America."

"I don't think you should have sent him away to school," Chris said.

"Maybe I shouldn't have."

"Because you can't properly love someone you never see."

"Do you think so?" Grandmother asked her. "I think it's a great deal harder to love someone you see all the time."

"Why?" Jackie asked.

"Because their faults are under your nose to sniff at every day, and you tend to take their good points for granted."

Chris looked at her grandmother, who was looking at her, not at Jackie. The gray eyes had a message, but Chris couldn't read it. "My father doesn't have any faults," Chris said. "He is the nicest man in the world."

"And your mother?" Grandmother asked her.

"Mother's all right when she's not picking on me or yelling about something."

"Does she always yell and pick on you?"

"Always lately," Chris said. "Anyway ever since . . . she used to be nice."

"Before your father left her?"

"May I borrow the silver coach for a while?" Chris asked, determined not to let Grandmother pry any more secrets out of her.

"Just be sure you put it back here on the shelf when you're finished using it. I would hate to lose it most of all the things I own."

"Thank you for lending it to me," Chris said. Then she walked out of the room, carrying the coach with her.

"Where are you going, Chrissie?" Jackie called after her.

"Upstairs to write some letters. I'd like to be alone for a while, Jackie."

"But who will I play with?" Jackie asked.

"You can come for a ride on the tractor with me while I mow the lawn," Grandmother said.

6

A small window in the attic looked out toward the mountains. Chris drew a fat blue hassock up to the window and surrounded herself with packing boxes so that she had a private closet all to herself. She brushed away a spider's web and set the coach up on the window sill where it gleamed in the sunlight. She drew up a low box to rest her pad and pen on. Then a sadness took the strength from her hand so that she could not write, and nothing to say came into her head.

She had been so disappointed when Daddy had not come as he promised on her birthday. It had been the worst thing that ever happened to her. But even when he had disappointed her so much, she had understood and forgiven him. It had all been Mother's fault—that all-day argument they had the week before the birthday about the stupid washing machine not working and how much it cost to repair it. That was why he hadn't come.

Chris toyed with the doors on the silver coach. They opened and shut on hinges, and there was a seat inside. But the coach was just a pretty ornament. Silly of

41

Grandmother to pretend it was magic. She must think Chris was a baby like Jackie, ready to believe such fairytales. Only, how to explain the tingle . . .

The warmth of the sun caressed Chris's forehead, almost as relaxing as her mother's hand was when she felt sick. Chris tried to focus on the shadows that moved slowly across the mountains' sides, but she felt too sleepy, too sleepy to keep her eyes open. She rubbed one finger lightly over the wire design of the coach's roof, resting on the pillow of her thoughts and the warm sunshine. The faint tingling sensation grew; it was definitely there now. All at once the coach began to shimmer. The air and the coach and everything shimmered and rippled and began to expand. The coach grew large so rapidly that it would have filled the attic from floor to ceiling—if Chris had been in the attic. But, quite unexpectedly, she found herself standing outside on the grass.

When the coach was full size, the shimmering stopped and everything fell reassuringly into place. The coach stood on the green lawn with the birds calling and the trees and the mountains standing just as they should be. The door in front of Chris swung open. Promptly, with no fear at all, she stepped up into the coach and sat down on the wire bench. As she blinked her eyes, two milk-white horses with swishing tails and tossing manes appeared. Black harnesses attached the horses to the coach, which took off with a jolt that made Chris grab hold of the window frame.

She could hear the sound of the horses' hoofbeats and feel the wind fingering her hair. Then the clop clop of the hoofs faded into silence, but the sense of speed, the feeling of pushing through the weight of the air, did not. She looked down through the fancy, wirework floor and saw that they had lifted right off the earth and were sailing through the blue sky as fast as a jet plane, as fast as a comet, and higher and higher until they had lifted over the mountain peaks and were just under the white puffs of clouds. Below, Chris saw the patched brown and green fields of the farms they had passed in the car yesterday. The coach was taking her toward home, and yet not quite home.

Excitement zinged through her as she realized the coach was taking her to Lake George in New York State, to the very same lakeside amusement park she had asked her father to take her to for her birthday. And so fast! Before her first joy had quite fizzled, she felt the settling, like sinking into soft cushions, as the coach and horses drifted to earth in a clearing among the trees near the parking lot.

When the coach door swung open, Chris jumped down, wondering if her coach was safely hidden. Then she realized that it had to be invisible to everyone else. Otherwise gaping crowds of people would now be rushing over to see the gleaming, lacy coach and the marvellous, matched white horses. She laughed and ran off into the parking lot, where she saw without surprise that her father was just getting out of his new yellow sportscar.

"Chris!" He swept her up into his arms and hugged her. "I'm sorry I missed your birthday treat. But now I'm here. Will you go to the amusement park with me—just you and me this time?"

"Oh yes! When Mother took me with Jackie it wasn't too good," she confided. "Mother kept worrying about how much everything cost, and she made me take Jackie on baby rides even though it was *my* birthday."

"Today it will be just the way you want it, Chris, my darling Christina Victoria Wallace."

First they rode the Wild Mouse and lost the bottoms

of their stomachs and found them again while screaming. Then they banged into each other in a wild chase in
the bumper cars, whose soft rubber fenders absorbed the
shock. Next they plummeted like diving birds in the
Loop-the-Loop, whipped round and whirled until they
were dizzy on the Tilt-a-Whirl.

"May I have a humongous cone of pink cotton candy?"
Chris asked. Her mother never let her buy the sweet,
cloudlike mass because she said it ruined your teeth.

"As much as you can eat," he said.

They rode every ride in the park, and got bumped,
swiveled, pitched, dropped, jerked, tumbled, whirled,
and agitated until they had had enough. Chris laughed
and shrieked more than she ever had in her entire life.
Even though she was not scared, her father held her
hand tight through it all.

Finally, at dusk, as the Ferris wheel they were riding
dipped slowly toward the lake, they watched the lights
of the little cabins hidden in the trees spark into life.
The lake was pearl gray and still, and the sky was tinged
with pink and green.

"Isn't it beautiful, Daddy?" Chris asked.

"Beautiful," Daddy agreed.

"Do you wish anybody was here with us?"

"No, Chris. I like it best with just you."

"I like being with you best too, Daddy."

"You're so sweet. You're a real sweetheart, Christina
Victoria Wallace. Now, would you like me to win some
prizes for you?"

"Yes, please."

He shot at moving ducks on a wire string and won an
enormous black-and-white stuffed panda. He threw base-
balls at a rubber head and won an Instamatic camera.
He pitched pennies into baskets and won a cameo ring.

Then he bought Chris a supper of hotdogs and soft ice cream, and she played bingo and won a pipe for him. By then the moon was out and something told her the coach was waiting.

"It's been the most wonderful birthday I ever had, even if it did come late," Chris said.

"I'm glad, Chris. I wanted it to be wonderful for you."

"I miss you so much, Daddy."

"Well, we'll see what we can do to fix that. As soon as I find a place to stay, you can come to live with me."

"Hurry, Daddy. Mother doesn't really like me, and Jackie won't miss me much."

"I'll try my best. You be good now."

"I'm always good—except sometimes when I say mean things, but I don't mean to be mean, if you know what I mean."

"I know what you mean. I love you." And he put his arms around her and kissed her goodbye.

She ran to the coach and piled in with all her prizes spilling from her arms. The horses took off so fast that she barely had time to wave goodbye to her father before she was back in Grandmother's house.

Not until she was sitting on the hassock in the attic, and the coach had returned to its normal size, did she find that she had mislaid her prizes. A disappointment. But, she consoled herself, at least she had the most marvelous day of her life to remember.

"Chris, where are you?" Jackie called.

"I'm here, Jackie." Chris stuck her hand up and waved so that Jackie could find her in the packing-case closet.

"Grandma and me looked all over and couldn't find you."

"You shouldn't say 'me.' You should say 'I,' "
Chris said, just as her mother would.

"Were you here all this time?"

"No. I was away in the silver coach."

"Oh . . . We found some baby rabbits in the grass
where we mowed. Grandma says if their mother doesn't
come back for them, I can keep them. Come see, Chris."

"Okay." Chris followed Jackie to the edge of the
woods, where a clump of tall grass hid a soft, brown
mass of baby rabbits all cuddled together in a grassy
nest. Chris spotted a pair of fingering ears and reached
down to pick the rabbit up, but Jackie said sharply,
"No, don't! Grandma said if you touch them, the mother's sure not to come back—if she's still alive. I fed them
milk from an eyedropper and they ate carrot tops.
Grandma says Mabel has an old rabbit hutch she might
let me use."

"They're cute," Chris said. One bright brown eye
surveyed her fearlessly.

"Where did you go in the silver coach?" Jackie
asked.

"To see Daddy."

"Oh. Why didn't you take me with you?"

"I wanted to go alone, Jackie."

Jackie's lips turned down. "I shared my rabbits with
you," she said.

"But Jackie," Chris said, "this isn't the same. Don't
feel bad, please. Look, you're still a little girl, and I'm
twelve. You can't expect me to take you along wherever
I go. That wouldn't be fair, would it? Would it now?"

Jackie shrugged and sighed. "I guess not," she said
reluctantly. "But I like being with you, Chrissie."

"Let's go explore the island together then, okay?"

Jackie put her hand in Chris's, and they walked across

46

the mowed grass and over the small bridge built of peeled logs that arched up over the pond. A path led around the island, which was not much bigger than the attic. The island was thick with bushes. A single clump of birch and a pine tree stuck up in the center. A bullfrog chugged in the green, still pond. A bird whistled. Already the day with her father seemed long ago to Chris. It could have been a dream. Most likely it had been a dream. The coach could not really be magic. But she *had* been on the Ferris wheel with her father. She could still taste the cotton candy, and she still felt happy. All that was real. Maybe the magic was real too.

"Can you show me how to make the coach go?" Jackie asked.

"I don't know. I think maybe you have to do it yourself, Jackie." Chris squeezed her sister's hand consolingly.

The sky was bleaching out toward evening. It was the time of day when nothing was certain and everything was strange. "Let's go see if Grandma needs help making dinner," Chris said, feeling guilty because Jackie looked sad.

7

Rain hummed on the roof in a busy rhythm. Chris sat up in bed and looked over at Jackie, who was still rolled up in sleep like a snail. Outside the dim attic, the pond looked gloomy. Raindrops pocked its black surface, and no sky, only a grayness, hovered over the lush green of the trees and grass. Chris slipped out of bed and into her housecoat. She padded downstairs to the warm, lighted kitchen where her grandmother sat curled around a cup of coffee, reading a magazine.

Usually in the morning, Jackie bounced into the kitchen first and threw her arms around their grandmother, giving her a hug and a kiss so enthusiastic that Chris's greeting always seemed second-rate by comparison. This morning Chris was first. She kissed her grandmother on the cheek, said a quiet good morning, and felt satisfied with herself.

"What are you reading?" Chris asked.

"A natural history magazine. I'm a natural history buff, I guess. I was looking through my journal last night and found I have more entries in it about animals

48

than about people. Pages and pages about things like a mongoose crossing the road or a little wren chasing a sparrow from a nesting site. That's queer, isn't it?''

"Why? You must just like animals."

"I do, but people matter more to me. You'd think I'd write more about them."

"Our teacher made us keep a journal in English last year. I wasn't very good at it. It's embarrassing to write things down." Chris assembled her own breakfast of juice, cereal, and milk.

"Embarrassing?" Grandmother repeated. "Yes, I suppose that's it. You've put your finger on it, Chris. It *is* embarrassing to expose your impolite thoughts on paper."

"Especially if some teacher's going to read it," Chris said.

"You're a very private person, aren't you?"

"I don't know . . . I can tell things, private things. I just hate writing what I think."

"Is that why you keep putting off answering your mother's letters?"

"I write to her," Chris said defensively.

"Not very often," Grandmother said.

"Jackie tells Mother everything in all those letters she dictates to you that you write for her. There's nothing left for me to write." Chris stiffened with resentment under the criticism, unwilling to admit she just didn't feel like writing to her mother and too polite to say it was none of her grandmother's business in any case.

"But how you see something is bound to be different from the way Jackie sees it. Your mother might like to know your reactions as well as Jackie's."

"All Mother cares about is if I'm behaving myself and if I'm well."

"Is that all?" Grandmother smiled.

"That's all," Chris said soberly, refusing to smile back.

"What makes you so sure?"

"That's all she ever asks me about."

"Maybe she's shy about asking you personal things."

"Mother's not shy."

"No? When I first met her, she struck me as very shy, a person who finds it hard to express her feelings."

"Why do you care about my mother?" Chris burst out. "You're Daddy's mother, not hers."

"I care about your mother because she's part of the family and the mother of my granddaughter, and I care a lot about you."

Chris thought about that. She didn't exactly understand, but she had a sense that her grandmother meant well, and it was nice to hear that Grandmother cared about her. "Maybe I'll write Mother today," Chris said.

"Rainy days are good letter-writing days," Grandmother said cheerfully. "You could sit at the kitchen table to hear the rain come down while you think of what to say." The wide-apart eyes, clear as water, studied Chris above the rim of the coffee cup. "You know," Grandmother said, "your father takes care of himself first, before anybody else gets taken care of— always has, most likely always will. Your mother, on the other hand, strikes me as a lady nobody's cared about enough . . . Am I wrong?"

Chris thought about her mother and tried to be fair. "Mother tries very hard to take care of us and to keep the house nice . . . and then she's been working part-time since Jackie started school. So she gets tired . . . And sometimes she's crabby when things don't go right. Little things. She loses her temper and she slaps me—me,

50

not Jackie, because Jackie's the baby. But if she's not tired, she's okay. She's never really fun like Daddy, though. She's too careful. Everything has to look just right and be just so. She's fussy.'' Chris remembered how her mother, looking tired after a day on her feet at the hospital, would go into her bedroom at six o'clock when the dinner was on the stove to put on makeup and comb her hair, so that she would look pretty when their father got home. She had been pretty once, probably, but their father never seemed to notice. Of course, he had not lived at home for almost a year now. A tendril of sympathy for her mother uncurled in her chest. Her mother probably didn't like being picky any more than Chris liked being mean.

''Grandmother,'' Chris said. ''Do you think people can ever be like they want to be even if they're not the way they want to be really?''

Grandmother smiled. ''You don't please yourself very much, do you?''

''Sometimes I do.''

''When?''

''When I'm dancing or when I'm with my father. I'd like myself if I were nice to Jackie all the time. If I were sweet . . . But I don't feel like being sweet most of the time.''

Grandmother said very firmly, ''Christina Victoria Wallace, for what it's worth, and it seems to be worth a good deal to you, you *are* sweet. You are sweet and you have lots of good qualities. Do you know I'm very proud of you?''

Chris flushed. Then she moved into her grandmother's open arms and gave her a hug as warm and loving as Jackie's ever was.

''You know what else today would be good for?''

51

Grandmother asked. "Today would be a good day for fixing up a tent in the attic."

"The tent! Oh yes, that would be fun."

"I have a whole trunkful of old bedspreads we could use, and a lot of laundry line. Let's go to it after breakfast."

Jackie bounded downstairs, gave Grandmother her hug-and-kiss special, and said, "Can I bring my rabbits inside so they don't catch cold in the rain?"

"I doubt that that's necessary," Grandmother said. "But since you've been so good about keeping them clean, and even changed their litter every day, I guess we can tolerate rabbits in the kitchen for a while."

"I'll help you carry the box in," Chris offered. She disliked going out in the rain, but she felt like being nice to Jackie for a change.

The rabbit hutch weighed a million tons. The four babies who had survived, even though their mother never came back to care for them, were thriving on twice-a-day feedings of milk, water, vegetables, and grass clippings, with rolled oats and melon rind thrown in for good measure on Mabel's advice. They set the box down under the coathooks next to the door.

"Can I let them hop around the kitchen floor?" Jackie asked.

"If you clean up their droppings."

"She's going to become a horse lover," Chris announced glumly. "I just know she is."

"And what's wrong with that?" Grandmother asked, looking amused.

"Nothing, except the horse-crazy girls I know are all weird. Who wants to go around mucking out stables and currying horses all the time except somebody who's weird?"

"Lots of people think horses are beautiful."

"Do you like horses especially, Grandmother?"

"Not any more than any other kind of animal. I like to look at them well enough when somebody else takes care of them, though."

"There you are," Chris said. "You're sensible, like me."

"I'm not weird," Jackie said.

"Okay," Chris said, "I'll give you a test. Which is more important, a baby rabbit or a baby human?"

"I don't know," Jackie said.

"Well, suppose they were both drowning. Which would you save?"

"I wouldn't save any," Jackie said, frowning.

"Why not?"

"I can't swim."

Grandmother laughed. Chris had to laugh too. "All right, Jackie, you pass," Chris said. "You're not weird."

Chris fondled a rabbit in her hands. It sat very still, except for tickling her chin with an occasional twitch of its ears. The kitchen was a nest of warmth and coffee smell, safe from the rain that was slashing at the windows and hammering on the roof.

Later Chris helped her grandmother carry the folding ladder up from the garage to the attic and held the ladder steady while Grandmother strung the nylon line in a big square around the posts nearest the beds. Grandmother nailed the line in place. "It'll probably sag some," she said, "but that shouldn't matter."

They took everything out of a box filled with castoff bedspreads and curtains and spread it out around the attic to consider. "It looks like a Moroccan bazaar," Grandmother said. It was Jackie who suggested the canopy overhead. They chose the white hobnail bed-

53

spread for the canopy because the fringe would look so pretty hanging down. At the windows they hung sheer white curtains draped in the middle. For the sides, Chris wanted the colorful, striped twin bedspreads. They were torn in places, so she and Grandmother sewed up the tears while Jackie danced around the attic, bedecked in a lace tablecloth and a fox fur hat. Finally, they decided that a sheer curtain at the open end would finish their square tent off cozily. Then nothing would do but they must all get on the beds under the tent with a bowl of fruit, a pan of fudge, and a deck of cards. All afternoon they played crazy eights and old maid and pig and giggled.

"This was the best day of my life," Jackie said.

"It was a lovely afternoon, and I like our tent," Chris said. Then she asked her grandmother, "When Daddy comes, where will he sleep?"

"On the couch in front of the fireplace. It opens into a bed."

"Did you write him we were here?"

"Yes."

"And when's he coming?"

"He isn't positive, he said, but he thinks maybe this Saturday coming up."

"So soon? Why didn't you tell us?"

"I didn't want you to be disappointed if something makes him change his plans."

"He could sleep up here if he likes our tent, and Jackie and I could sleep on the couch."

"I'm sure he won't be fussy about where he sleeps."

"I'm going to write my mother this afternoon," Chris said.

"Me too," Jackie said.

"Good," Grandmother said. "When you write, you

might ask her to visit us for a while when she finishes her school. A few days of quiet relaxing in the country should do her good, don't you think?''

Chris nodded, but she thought that it was quite likely she would be gone by then. Her father would be taking her back with him when he left after this weekend.

8

Mabel was coming to spend the whole afternoon. Chris and Jackie decided to plan some entertainment for her. Chris would dance and Jackie would sing. They had been alone so much that it was exciting to have a visitor, even if the visitor was only Mabel, who often stopped by for a few minutes after work.

Mabel had been Jackie's consultant on the care and feeding of baby rabbits. She had also tried to teach them how to fish in the pond, but when Chris's hook caught deep in the pretty, blue-green, flecked bluegill who stared at them with one black-centered, orange eye while Mabel tried to work the hook out, Chris lost interest in fishing. What Chris and Jackie liked to do best at the pond was feed the orange carp that waited for them under the bridge in the thick, greenish water. Feeding the fish, caring for the rabbits, making interesting things like the carrot bread Grandmother taught them how to bake for Mabel, playing endless games of monopoly and cards, swimming at the lake Grandmother drove them to on warm afternoons, climbing in the huge, old, double-trunked pine, writing letters, reading aloud from *Alice in Wonderland,* all those things and more—the come-quick sight of a scarlet cardinal on the bird feeder, the perky-eared fox they glimpsed—filled the days with so much activity that they had little time left for homesickness. They did not even miss the companionship of other children. Still, Chris could hardly wait until her father came. He slipped into her mind from all the corners of her thoughts. Her real life would begin when he came.

"Look what I found!" Jackie called, running down the open steps from the attic just as Chris finished tucking daisies and buttercups into a blue dish on the table, where the carrot bread and coffee cups waited for Mabel.

Jackie was holding a pleated slip with a frill around the bottom. "Where did you find it?" Chris asked.

"In a suitcase upstairs. Wouldn't it make a good dancing costume for you, Chris?"

"Too long," Chris said. "It would come down to my ankles."

"But you could tie a string around the middle and wear it way up high."

Chris considered. Jackie was so bright sometimes. "Maybe I'll try it and see how it looks. Thanks, Jackie." Chris had planned to tie a scarf around her bathing suit and dance in that. The slip might make a better costume. "You can have the black scarf to wear for your costume if the slip works," Chris offered.

"Can I? Oh thank you, Chrissie."

They got dressed in Grandmother's bedroom, where they could use the mirror. Mabel was out in the kitchen telling Grandmother the latest news about her unlucky daughter. Chris tied a red sash around the middle of the white slip and thought it made a lovely costume. If only she had her ballet slippers! She pirouetted in front of the mirror and caught a glimpse over one shoulder of a slender, graceful dancer. It was only full face that she was just Chris in a slip, pretending. "I wish Grandmother had some makeup we could use," Chris said, and wished too that her father could see how she looked.

"Do I look pretty?" Jackie asked. She had the black lace scarf tied clumsily around her middle and was trying to manipulate the Spanish fan. Chris retied the scarf for her, draping it over one shoulder and tying it under her arm.

"You'd look better if you didn't have your jeans underneath. Don't you have a skirt with you?"

"No," Jackie said.

"Maybe you could wear the ruffled party apron that Mabel made for Grandmother."

The apron went around Jackie one and a half times, making a wrap skirt that delighted Jackie, and Chris too, because she had thought of it.

"You look beautiful," Chris said. Jackie threw her arms around her sister and kissed her. Chris was embarrassed. "Jackie, you're yucky."

Chris hid her finery under her grandmother's housecoat and went out to make sure the stage was set for her dance. She put Stravinsky's *Firebird Suite* on the hi-fi, instructed the two ladies to sit on the couch and be ready, and ran back into the bedroom. She handed the housecoat to Jackie, who wrapped it around herself to cover her costume and pranced out to sit on the couch between Mabel and Grandma and be the third member of Chris's audience.

Chris waited in the kitchen behind the fireplace for a good place in the music, then began. "*Glissade,*" she told herself, "and one, and two." She went gliding out

58

with her arms arched over her head. In the center of the room, in front of the fireplace, she stood holding her position for four beats, then made a *grand plié* and another and did some of the quick little trembly steps called *pas de chats* that Mrs. Jason said she did particularly well. Then, carried far beyond her knowledge by the powerful music, she gave way to invention and made up swooping, swaying, dipping motions to accompany the rhythms. She felt beautiful as she leaped and bent and stretched and flexed her slender body. She lost herself in the sheer joy of the dancing. The enthusiastic cries of praise from Grandmother and Mabel at the end, when she sank into her *révérence,* came at her like distant waves rolling into her quiet shore.

"Just lovely," Mabel gasped, wiping her eyes. "Just like on TV. Just the prettiest ballet dancer I ever seen. Why, I never imagined you could dance that pretty, a little girl like you!"

"That was lovely, Chris," Grandmother said when she finished clapping, and Mabel had stopped for breath. "Thank you for the entertainment."

"And don't that slip make a good costume!" Mabel said.

"When I saved that frivolous thing," Grandmother said, "I never dreamed it would be a dancer's costume someday. It was lovely."

"Jackie thought of it," Chris said. She settled down on the couch in Jackie's place, still caught up in the happy spray of praise.

Jackie discarded her housecoat and took centerstage in front of the fireplace, wrestling with the fan and the shawl, which kept slipping. The audience sat smiling expectantly, quiet now. All of a sudden Jackie realized everyone was watching her. She blushed and giggled—she who showed off as naturally as she breathed.

"Jackie, don't be silly," Chris admonished her. "It's just us."

Jackie giggled some more, tried to start singing, then ran and hid her head in a chair cushion. She acted so silly that Chris got disgusted with her. "What is wrong with you?" Chris demanded.

Jackie tried again and lost herself in giggles.

"You always ruin everything," Chris said, as cross as her mother got when things went wrong.

"I do not," Jackie protested. Tears immediately replaced the giggles.

"Chris, don't jump on her. We have plenty of time," Grandmother said.

"Well, not forever," Chris said. "Come on, Jackie, sing!"

"I don't want to sing now," Jackie whimpered and crumpled up in the chair, all wet, hurt feelings.

Chris felt Mabel's and Grandmother's reproachful eyes on her. With a great sigh of impatience, she went to put her arms around Jackie and soothe her. Coaxed and cuddled, Jackie finally sang. She had a sweet, clear voice that wavered only a little when she ran too high up the scale. She sang "This Land Is Your Land." Grandmother and Mabel made just as much fuss over Jackie's singing as they had over Chris's dancing. Chris thought her act had been better, but she understood that they did not want to hurt Jackie's feelings.

That evening, when Grandmother was reading one of the many magazines that she said kept her in touch with the world, Chris curled up on the couch with the silver coach. If it were really magic, she thought, it would make a miracle for her. If it were really magic—if only it were!

She closed her eyes, her fingers tracing the wire flower design in the coach's roof. Her hands tingled. The shimmering began. Then the coach expanded as fast as a balloon reaching full size. The horses appeared, familiar now. But this time, when the shimmering stopped and the world returned to normal, Chris found herself standing outside next to the coach on a starlit night. She was dressed in a spangled white tutu, and her fingers told her the weight on her head was a tiara. She gasped with delight and stepped up into the coach, which lifted off at once into the dark, star-hung night.

The wind was warm. All around Chris felt the swishing dark. All she could see was the stars and the luminescent tails of the horses flowing toward her like heatless flames. She sat still, transfixed by the beauty of it all, until the coach suddenly began to descend, and she saw below her the well-lighted lawns of the Saratoga Performing Arts Center. People were sitting about on blankets, attending to the stage as if a performance were going on. The coach passed under the open shell of the theater itself and over the heads of the audience seated inside. It landed right on the stage. The stage was empty except for Chris, the coach, and a backdrop painted with imitation twinkling stars and false snowbanks. The audience breathed like a murmurous sea beyond the footlights.

Chris stepped down onto the stage and found herself in the spotlight. She looked down at herself, at her spangled white tutu and white tights and satin toeshoes. Exquisite! Her chin lifted proudly. Light as a butterfly, she rose into an arabesque, her weight on one foot, her arms curves of grace. The audience applauded expectantly, then stilled. She stood there forever, never wavering until the music of Debussy sent her dreaming, soft as a floating snowflake, around the stage.

She danced. She danced as if she were a prima ballerina. She danced with the fairy grace she had seen when her mother took her to see Patricia McBride performing in *Coppelia*. She danced in the hushed hall for as long as the music carried her. Afterwards, above the roar of the audience applauding her, she heard her father's voice shouting, "Bravo! Bravo, Christina Victoria Wallace, bravo!" When she raised her head, the stage was filled with roses. Her handsome father, in white tails with a red carnation in his lapel, leaped down from his box to join her on the stage.

"My darling daughter, you were wonderful. I never knew you could dance so beautifully."

"Daddy," Chris said. "Let's fly away together in my silver coach, just you and me."

"Of course, Christina," he said. With his hand clasped in hers, she gave a last wave to her cheering audience and led her father into the coach. As soon as they were seated, the coach lifted off and flew over the heads of the audience, out over the lawns, and up into the dark blue sky.

"When I grow up, I'm going to be a ballerina," Chris said as the quiet night enveloped them, leaving only the soft whoosh of their passage.

"Of course you are, Christina. I'll send you to a ballet school in New York, and whenever you dance, I'll be in the audience to watch you."

"I love you, Daddy."

"And I love you, Christina."

Her grandmother's hand on her shoulder woke Chris up. "You fell asleep here on the couch," Grandmother said. "Better go on up to bed now. I'm turning in myself."

"Oh," Chris said. "Was I asleep?" She sat up. The silver coach had fallen to the floor. She picked it up. "It was just a dream then?"

"Were you dreaming?"

"I was on the stage at the Saratoga Performing Arts Center."

"That must have been a lovely dream."

"But it was real. It could have been real. You said the coach was magic."

"It is—for me."

"It's magic for me too," Chris said.

"You think you were really there then?"

"Maybe I was."

"Well, anything's possible."

"Is it possible, Grandmother?"

"Dreams come true sometimes, and then there are dreams that are so much like reality that it's hard to tell the difference."

"Do you really believe in magic, Grandmother?"

"I believe our minds are full of magic, but most of us don't know how to use it. You're lucky if you know how to make the silver coach go. I hope you never lose that ability, Chris." She kissed Chris lightly and sent her off to bed.

9

All morning Jackie and Chris kept running to the road to see if their father was coming yet. "It won't make him get here any faster," Grandmother said. "You're going to wear yourselves out before he comes."

But it was impossible to hold back their excitement, even though they each had enough to do preparing home-baked bread and pies and cleaning vegetables and salad for the lunch and dinner they had planned especially to please him.

"Can we have candles on the table?" Chris asked as she chopped up the onions, a job her grandmother hated because it irritated her eyes so much.

"For lunch? It'll be too light out, won't it?"

"All right, just for dinner then. Jackie, did you get the daisies down by the road to go with those blue flowers from Grandmother's garden?"

"Oh no. I'll get them now." Jackie ran off.

Chris asked, "Grandmother, what are you smiling at?"

"You—blue delphiniums and white daisies. Where did you get your eye for flower arranging?"

"Mother always makes flower arrangements for the table when we have company."

"Does she? That's nice. I wish I knew your mother better. I remember when I met her—that was before you were born—she was so shy that she just sat there and let your father do all the talking. I guess I wasn't too good at putting her at her ease."

"She's not shy any more, I don't think." Chris considered her mother a minute. Was she shy? Sometimes she acted nervous about little things, like telling the cleaner about the spots on Daddy's shirts, or the time she threw up the morning she was going for her job interview. Maybe Mother did get scared about things, but she never said so. The only thing she ever said was, "You didn't vacuum under the beds, Chris. You forgot to lock the door, Chris. Must you have your elbow on the table when you eat, Chris? Why can't you be nice and let Jackie be with you and your friends? Don't you care about anybody but yourself, Chris? Can't you ever say anything nice to anybody, Chris? Don't you understand how tired I am, Chris?"

Chris sighed and shut her mother out of her mind. Today her father was coming, and her whole life was going to change. She had packed all her clothes into her suitcase last night after Jackie fell asleep. It made her feel guilty with Jackie sleeping there so trustingly. Even though Chris knew Jackie was happy with Grandmother and happy at home with Mother, still, the guilt stuck. Of course, she could ask Daddy if he would take Jackie too. It wouldn't take long to pack Jackie's things. Chris hoped Grandmother wasn't going to be lonely when they left, but it was only a few more weeks until the end of the summer, when they would be going anyway. She would tell her father they really ought to visit Grandmother Wallace more, or have her come to visit them. Chris sighed again. Making everybody happy was so complicated.

"When is he coming?" Chris asked. It was almost noon, but no sounds of a car rumbling up the dirt road broke the shuffling of the wind through the treetops and the creaking of the insects in the heat of the August afternoon. "Napkins," Chris thought, and ran inside to set them out on the lunch table.

"I hear a car!" Jackie shrieked. Chris put down the last napkin and joined Grandmother at the door. Jackie was bouncing up and down where the road turned in to Grandmother's driveway. An old Ford station wagon with dented fenders, unfamiliar to Chris, rounded the last bend. Her father stepped out of the car on the driver's side; two boys somewhere in age between Jackie and Chris leaped out the back. Then a slender, smiling woman with long, dark hair got out the far side, holding the hand of a delicate little girl, smaller than Jackie, maybe three or four years old.

"Who are they?" Chris asked in dismay.

"I haven't the faintest idea," Grandmother said. She sounded angry.

Chris's father was grinning beautifully. With his square chin shorn of the beard he had the last time she saw him, he looked young and merry. He tossed Jackie up into the air and hugged her in greeting. "Jackie, my little gremlin, how are you doing?"

"Daddy, you gotta come and see my rabbits!" Jackie screeched in her excitement.

"I will, I will. Just let me say hello and introduce everybody. Chris, Mother!" he called. "Aren't you going to say hello?"

Chris went running into his arms as if everything she

66

could ever want was in them. "Oh Daddy, I'm so glad you're here!"

"Did you miss me, Puss?"

"Only every minute."

"I missed you too, sweetheart." He took one arm away from Chris, drew his mother to him, bent, and kissed her cheek.

"You're looking good, Mother."

"So are you, Don." She sounded cool. Chris looked at her in surprise. Didn't Grandmother like her own son?

"Mother, Chris, Jackie," he said as if he had not noticed his mother's coolness, "I want to introduce you to my friend Anne Maxwell. And these are her children, Buddy and Leroy, and this little trinket is Susie."

"My name's *not* Leroy," the freckle-faced redhead protested.

Chris's father snapped his fingers in mock dismay. "Oops, sorry, I forgot! It's Roy Lee, isn't it?"

"It's just *Roy*!" The redhead flushed at the teasing, making his cheeks and hair all one color.

"That's right! Roy, let me introduce you to my daughters, Christina Victoria and Jacqueline Marie. Aren't they beautiful?"

"They're girls," Roy said with disgust.

"I'll say they are!" their father said.

"Will you all be staying with us for dinner?" Grandmother asked.

"Now Mother, don't fuss. We just stopped by for a few hours. We'll eat dinner on the road on our way to New Hampshire."

Chris caught her grandmother's troubled gray eyes and begged her silently to make him stay.

67

"You misunderstood me, Don. We're all prepared for you to stay for both lunch and dinner."

"Not for a crew this size," he said, laughing. "I didn't warn you I was bringing three hungry cubs with me." He grabbed Buddy and Roy, one in each arm, and hung on while they tried to wrestle themselves loose. The boys working together laid him flat on his back on the grass. With howls of victory, they freed themselves.

"He's such a boy himself, isn't he?" Anne Maxwell said, smiling easily at Grandmother.

"I'd thought he was a man," Grandmother said.

When her father stood up, Chris moved to stand beside him and take his hand. "We have roast chicken with stuffing and a chocolate fudge cake for dinner," she pleaded.

"Don't make me feel bad for not staying, Puss. Come on, let's enjoy the time we have together."

Jackie, not used to being ignored, jumped up and down, swinging on his other arm. "Daddy, let me show you the rabbits, please!"

"All right, honey. We'll all go see the rabbits. What do you say, Susie? Want to see some real live Easter bunnies?"

Susie smiled shyly and clung to her mother.

"Quite a group we have here," Chris's father said with pride. "We could open our own elementary school."

"I'm going into the seventh grade, Daddy," Chris pointed out with dignity.

"So you are, so you are." He hugged her.

Chris clung to her father's hand as they walked, but an uneasy feeling was blotting out her joy. What were these people doing here? Why was he so friendly to those boys and that little girl? Why couldn't he stay?

Jackie opened the top of her rabbit cage and talked

about how big the babies had gotten and what she fed them and about the two that had died. Roy stuck some grass under the nose of the little one with the dark spot on its head, but it just retreated into the huddle of soft, rounded bodies until only its ears were showing.

"Where did you find them?" Buddy asked.

"In the tall grass over there when Grandma and me mowed the lawn," Jackie said.

"Can I pick one up?"

"Well," Jackie said, "okay, but you gotta hold them very carefully because they get scared when you pick them up." She showed him how to hold them with one hand under the rabbit's hindquarters and one on the back of the neck.

"Jackie is a faithful keeper," Grandmother said. "She never forgets to feed them and she cleans the cage out every day."

"Aren't they big enough to feed themselves yet?" Buddy asked.

"Probably not yet," Grandmother said. "In another week or two I expect they'll be able to make it on their own. Then Jackie will let them loose."

"Maybe I could keep one," Jackie said with longing.

"You'll have to see what your mother says," Grandmother said.

Chris was smiling up at her father. She wanted to get his assurance that he was taking her away with him today, but it did not seem like the time to ask, not with all these people around. She wished she had written the letter she had meant to write, so that it was all settled now instead of still having to be arranged. And, she realized, these people would be leaving with them. What were they to him? "My friend Anne Maxwell," he had said. That was odd. His friends had always been men or couples he and Mother had known together. Chris wanted to ask how long she had to wait until Anne Maxwell and her children went away and it would be just Chris and her father alone together, but it wasn't a polite question with the woman standing there.

"And what have you been doing with yourself all summer, Christina?" her father asked.

"Lots of things. Grandmother taught us to bake, Jackie and me. I can bake lots of things you like now, Daddy, and I know how to make preserves."

"Do you really, baby? That's terrific. I guess staying with your grandmother has been good for you."

"Grandmother's my favorite person next to you."

"Next to me, huh? How's your mother fit in there?"

Chris did not answer. She couldn't answer a question like that with these strangers listening.

"I think Susie needs to use a bathroom," Anne Maxwell said.

"I'll show you where it is," Grandmother said. "Chris, why don't you take your father down to the island and show him the red carp you and Jackie have been fattening up?"

"Hey!" Roy said, "an island? Can we come too?"

"Sure guys, the more the merrier," Chris's father said and led off with his arm around her. The boys ran ahead. In a minute Jackie had popped her rabbits back in their box and come running to fit herself under their father's other arm.

Chris rubbed her cheek against the back of her father's strong, hairy hand. She had so many things jumbled in her head to say to him that it was easier to be silent than to pick one to begin with. Jackie was telling him about some of their adventures.

" . . . and then Grandma said I could ride in the back

70

of the truck if I held on really tight, but she wouldn't let me do it on the bumpy part of the road, but when we got on the good road going to the lake, then she let me, and a bird flew right past my nose.''

"Daddy," Chris said dreamily, "you know Grandmother's silver coach?"

"What?" He looked down at her smiling, but too distracted by Jackie, who was pulling his arm and saying, "And Daddy—" to understand Chris.

"The silver coach Grandmother got when you went to school," Chris said.

"Oh that. Yes, what about it, honey?"

Chris felt a cold stone drop in her chest, a premonition of disaster, but her father didn't notice any change in her. They were standing on the bridge now.

"I saw a big red fish. Is that the carp?" Roy asked.

"They're orange," Jackie said. "And some are white."

"They look like giant goldfish. Can we catch them?"

"Of course not!" Jackie said in horror. "They're not fishy fish, they're—"

"Like pets," her father finished sympathetically.

Jackie nodded. Chris's mind, skittering about in confusion, turned up the immediate problem of her costume. If she was going to dance for her father this afternoon, she should get it off the line in back, where she had hung it to dry after washing it. "Daddy, let's go back to the house," she said.

"You go ahead, honey. We'll be along in a few minutes," her father said.

Reluctantly, she turned and headed back across the lawn toward the clothesline. Then it struck her. How could she dance in front of all these people? Maybe if she could get her father alone, but . . . Everything was so in pieces, and none of the pieces were the right fit for the picture she had in her head. She looked over her shoulder and shivered to see her father with the boys on one side of him and Jackie on the other side walking into the tiny wood on the island.

In the kitchen Grandmother was putting the coffeepot on the stove while Anne Maxwell sat at the table with her daughter on her lap.

"Chris!" Grandmother said. "Are you all right?"

"I'm okay," Chris said.

"You look pale." Grandmother stopped lighting the gas range and moved toward Chris as if she were going to touch her.

"Are you traveling with my father?" Chris asked Anne Maxwell.

"Traveling? Well, yes, in a way. We're going to New Hampshire for vacation," the woman said, smiling.

"Together? You're going together with my father?" Chris asked.

"Yes." Anne Maxwell said. Her smile faded.

Chris veered toward the stairs. "I don't feel too well," she said to her grandmother. It was true; she didn't.

Chris lay stomach down on her bed. Her eyes fixed on a spider building a web under the nightstand that separated Jackie's bed from hers. The spider had a whitish body and dingy legs. The web was nowhere near as beautiful as the ones on the grass in the morning with dewdrops still sparkling on them, but Chris watched for a long, long time, not thinking anything.

"Chris?" Her grandmother's voice was followed by the touch of her soft hand on Chris's shoulder. "We're ready to eat lunch. They're all downstairs."

"I'm not hungry."

"I don't think they plan to stay very long."

72

Chris shrugged and tried to stop hearing anything.

"If you miss the rest of his visit, you may feel sorry later."

"I don't feel well."

"Tell me, if you couldn't have a whole glass of water when you were thirsty, wouldn't a little sip be better than nothing?"

"I don't know."

"Well, you do what's best for you, darling." Grandmother patted her back and left. Chris could hear their voices downstairs. Everyone was talking at once in high, excited voices. She heard her father's laugh. The sound of it made her sit up, then stand up, then go downstairs.

"How are you feeling, Chris?" her father asked.

She sat down at the place they had left for her. "Fine," she said.

The little girl, Susie, was sitting on his lap drinking a glass of milk. Chris looked at her and didn't feel like eating anything. The boys were gobbling everything in sight, their hands reaching for more while they still had food in their open mouths.

"Look at these fellers go!" her father said. "They're storing up energy for that ballgame we're gonna play after lunch, I bet."

"What ballgame?" Roy asked.

"The touch football game I'm gonna beat you in."

"No, you're not," Roy said.

"Can I play?" Jackie asked.

"Sure you can, Jackie."

"Do you know how?" Buddy asked.

"No."

"Well, who's gonna teach her?" Buddy asked.

"Oh, come on, Buddy. Anyone who wants to can play. Wanna play, Anne?" Chris's father asked.

"No, thank you. I'll put Susie down for a nap. Then I'll help your mother with the dishes."

"Chris?"

"No, thank you, Daddy." She didn't like games like football. She had not realized that her father did. "Will there be time—" The rest of her question was erased by the distraction of Roy's spilled glass of milk. She had to get her father alone to explain how much she needed to live with him. She would make him take her for a walk in the woods—now.

The boys ran out to the car to get a football. Chris followed her father outside, taking his hand. "Daddy?"

"What, honey?" He looked down at her with his bright eyes tender.

"I need to talk to you alone for a while."

"Right now, Christina?"

"Yes, now."

"I promised the boys this football game, baby. Later maybe, okay?"

She felt a terrible loss, as if the wind had just blown her life away. When he saw her silent, he kissed the top of her head and said, "Come watch us if you don't want to play." He ran off onto the lawn where Jackie and the boys were waiting for him. Chris stood there for a few minutes. The two boys and her father chased each other on the grass with Jackie zigzagging about, getting in their way. In the kitchen Anne Maxwell had just returned from putting her daughter to sleep in Grandmother's bedroom. Grandmother was stacking dirty dishes and bringing them to the sink.

"Susie's exhausted, poor little thing, fell right to sleep. She's not used to so many hours of driving."

"Where are you going in New Hampshire?" Grandmother asked.

"We rented a cottage by a lake, sight unseen, through a friend. Don's going to teach the boys how to sail. They're so excited they can hardly wait. They think he's the greatest. He's so good with kids!"

Chris stepped into the kitchen and saw her grandmother looking at Anne Maxwell with that far-seeing look. "Perhaps he's good with other people's," Grandmother said. Anne Maxwell looked startled; her eyes flicked to Chris and back to Grandmother again, then down at the floor.

"I'd better go outside and see what they're up to out there," Anne Maxwell said and hurried out.

Grandmother slapped the dishrag down on the counter and said, "I'm sorry, Chris. I shouldn't have made you come downstairs."

"I don't understand, Grandmother," Chris said. She picked up the dishtowel. She didn't want an explanation, and her grandmother didn't offer one.

"No," Grandmother said. "We'll let the dishes go. I'll do them tonight after they're gone."

They went out to the stoop and sat down side by side to watch the ballgame. Chris's father was dashing about with the boys and Jackie as if he was having as good a time as they were. He had never suggested playing ball with Chris that she could remember. She had an eerie sense of dislocation, as if Roy and Buddy were Daddy's sons and Susie, who had sat on his lap at lunch, were his daughter, while she and Jackie were outsiders. What had happened to their family? How could he become somebody else's father when he had been hers for twelve years? Hadn't he said he loved her best? Sometimes he forgot things, but he couldn't forget that.

She waited patiently until the ballgame ended. "Okay, you guys," her father said. "Disappear for a while now. It's time for the adults to have a gab session." Jackie stood poised like a sparrow ready to fly off but not knowing in which direction. The boys ran off together toward the bridge to the island. On his way into the house, her father rubbed the top of Chris's head in passing, casually, the way he would pat a dog's head. He sat down at the cleared kitchen table. Anne Maxwell sat next to him. Grandmother stood at the sink piled with dirty dishes. Jackie dragged over to Chris and sat down on the step beside her, leaning her head wearily against her sister's arm. Chris shrugged her off.

"Stop it, Jackie. Don't pester me now." Chris wanted to listen. She would give them a chance to talk and then beg again for just a few minutes. Then she would explain to him plainly that she wanted to live with him, not with her mother.

"You're going through with the divorce then," Grandmother said.

"Definitely. Mary wants it as much as I do now," he said.

"And your girls?" Grandmother asked.

"My girls will always have a father just as they have a mother."

"But you won't be living with them."

"Well, Mother, that doesn't seem to be a prerogative of parenthood, does it? You managed to raise me without living with me, didn't you?"

"Chris needs you," Grandmother said.

"Chris and Jackie will always be welcome to visit us. Won't they, Anne?"

"Of course," Anne Maxwell said.

Chris did not allow the rest of their conversation to

filter through her concentration. She was rehearsing exactly what she would say to him. "Daddy, come for a walk with me, please. I have to talk to you in private." Just a few minutes was all she needed. He was such a kind man. All she had to do was tell him. Then everything would be all right.

"Chrissie," Jackie whispered. "Why are those people with Daddy?"

"I don't know."

"But why are they here?"

"Because they're going on vacation together." Now was the right time, she decided. Now. She stood up abruptly and walked into the kitchen. The only person there was Grandmother, sitting at the table with her hands folded and her head down.

"Where did Daddy go?" Chris asked.

"He's in the bathroom. They seem to be in a hurry to leave, Chris. They want to get to New Hampshire before dark. Call Jackie to come say goodbye."

Anne Maxwell came out of Grandmother's bedroom holding a sleepy little girl in her arms. "Thanks for the lunch, Mrs. Wallace," Anne Maxwell said. "I'm so glad I had a chance to meet you."

"Yes," Grandmother said vaguely, not looking at her.

"Daddy," Chris said when he came out of the bathroom. "Daddy, *please* come for a walk with me. I need to talk to you for a minute."

"Sorry, honey, no time this trip." He bent and gave her a consoling kiss. "We've got a long way to go still. How about you write me a letter and tell me all about it, whatever it is. Okay?"

"Daddy, can Chris and me come with you to New Hampshire?" Jackie asked from the doorway.

77

"Not this time, gremlin. Your mother wouldn't like it. Once Anne and I have settled down, you girls can come to visit with us. Okay?"

"But Daddy," Jackie said. "Aren't you coming home to our family?"

Everyone froze for an instant as if Jackie had brought some painfully embarrassing object out of hiding and made them look at it. Then they whisked her question out of sight with a flurry of activities: "Where did the boys get to?" . . . "Did everyone use the bathroom before we leave?" . . . "Almost forgot to give you the box of candy we brought you, Mother." . . . "Goodbye, goodbye, goodbye." . . .

Jackie did not start to cry until the boys had been packed into the car along with Anne and her daughter, and the car had disappeared down the road. Once she did start to cry, though, she could not seem to stop.

"Jackie," Chris said finally, in desperation. "Don't the rabbits have to be fed?"

"Good girl," Grandmother muttered to Chris as Jackie's tears evaporated in the heat of her responsibility. Jackie took the lettuce Grandmother had saved for her and trudged off to her rabbits.

"Want me to call Mabel up to help us eat the dinner we prepared for tonight?" Grandmother asked.

"No," Chris said.

"Maybe you're right. I could freeze most of it and use it when your mother comes. We could make it a graduation dinner for her. She might like that."

"Grandmother," Chris said. "Why did you tell me the silver coach was magic when it's not?"

"Isn't it?" Grandmother asked. "I thought it was magic for you, just the way it is for me."

"No. It's just a lie."

78

"Did I lie to you?"

"I don't know." All she knew was that she hurt. She hurt so much from the torn-out place where she used to think her father loved her best. She hurt too much for tears, and much too much for comforting.

10

They were still in the kitchen when they heard Jackie's screams. Chris arrived first at the rabbit box where Jackie was standing.

"What's wrong? What's happened, Jackie?" Chris shook her sister, who stopped screaming but could not speak. Chris looked at the box. The rabbits were gone.

"Someone left the cover off," Grandmother said.

"I closed it. I always close it," Jackie said.

"Maybe one of the boys came back to look at the rabbits again and left the box open by mistake," Grandmother said.

"They're all going to die now," Jackie said.

"Not necessarily. We don't really know for sure; they might be perfectly able to survive by themselves right now."

"We'll go look for them," Chris said. "Maybe we can get them back in the box. Come on, Jackie. Let's go all around the lawn and the edge of the woods."

"Good idea," Grandmother said. "We'll each cover a different part of the yard."

They searched the lawn carefully. Chris knew it was hopeless right from the start, but she thought the searching might calm Jackie down. A small brown rabbit could so easily hide in the ragged grass or blend into the bushes. They pried apart the overgrown planting around the base of the house and found asparagus stalks three feet high, but no rabbits. They poked into the brush that fringed the woods where the mown grass stopped and scared a garter snake which zipped away. They looked particularly hard in the vegetable garden and around the lake. The sun had melted into a golden globe just above the mountains. The sky was milk glass.

"I bet they'll be all right, Jackie," Grandmother said when they could no longer tell a rabbit from a rock or a clod of earth. "If they can disappear so completely, they probably *are* ready to take care of themselves in the woods."

Jackie didn't answer. Silence was so odd in her that Chris and Grandmother watched her anxiously. All through supper, which was scrambled eggs with tomatoes, onions, and green peppers, Jackie was silent. She ate her share, but she would not even look at them.

"Jackie," Chris said. "Want to play cards with me?"

Jackie shook her head no.

"How about if we start reading *The Hobbit* tonight?" Grandmother suggested.

"I don't feel like it," Jackie said.

In bed that night, when Chris heard Jackie crying softly to herself, the pain of the visit that had promised to be so wonderful and had turned out so miserable sprouted in Chris. She slid into her sister's bed and put her arms around her.

"Listen," Chris said. "It's all right. The rabbits will be all right in the woods."

81

Jackie sobbed. "Daddy doesn't love us any more."

"Oh yes, he does. He still loves us," Chris said, holding Jackie tight. "He just doesn't love us best." Then the hot tears burst out of Chris too, and she and Jackie clung to each other and wept.

11

Three days passed and still Chris hurt. Was the hurt going to stick in her for her whole life, she wondered, and she asked her grandmother, "When your daughter died, how long did it take you to feel all right again?"

"Sometimes when I think about her, it still aches," Grandmother said, "and she's been dead over a year now. But the worst part, when I felt it every day and night, that took, oh I don't know, maybe a few weeks. Less than I'd expected really."

Chris nodded. She hoped she was not going to feel this way for weeks, but if she had to, she could survive it. It helped that she had Jackie to take care of. Jackie seemed to have suffered as much as Chris had, whether over the rabbits or their father Chris did not know, but she tried to keep Jackie too busy to brood, and that kept Chris too busy to sink into her own misery.

On Thursday of that week, Mabel came. She hailed them cheerfully when they were at the breakfast table, "Anybody home?"

"Just us," Grandmother answered. "Come have a cup of coffee with us, Mabel."

"Don't mind if I do. Brought you a half a watermelon. Charley and me are eating our way through the other half and getting sick of it. Do you like watermelon, Jackie?"

"Yes," Jackie said, and took her dishes to the sink. "Can I go now, Grandma?"

"Sure, honey. Go ahead."

"What's the matter with her?" Mabel asked Chris when Jackie had gone outside.

"She's been feeling sad since my father was here," Chris said.

"Oh, that's right. You had a visitor this past weekend, didn't you? How was it?" She helped herself to three spoons of sugar from the bowl and stirred it into her coffee, looking at Chris for an answer.

Chris shrugged. "Jackie's rabbits all got loose."

"Oh," Mabel said. "And that's what she's down in the mouth about?"

"Donald came with friends," Grandmother said. "A young woman and her three children."

"Didn't give you any warning?" Mabel asked.

"None," Grandmother said. "It shook us all up."

"Spoiled the day?"

"In spades. Jackie's been moping ever since, and Chris, as mature as she is, is feeling jilted. At least I suspect that's how she's feeling."

Chris looked at Grandmother with respect. She had not realized her grandmother understood her feelings that well without even needing to ask about them. "Mature," Grandmother had called her. Chris wondered when she had suddenly gotten mature. Maybe that had come along with the breasts that she had noticed were

84

definitely appearing, swelling out her T-shirt where it had not swelled before.

"My father's got a new family instead of us," Chris said, meaning to be cool, but the words choked her so that her voice sounded broken.

"Now I don't know about that," Mabel said. "I can't believe in his heart he'd ever put somebody else's kids in place of his own daughters. Right, Eve?"

"They've got a right to be upset," Grandmother said. "He acted badly. My son is a charming man who doesn't understand anybody's feelings but his own."

Chris thought of her mother, startled to realize she had not imagined how hurt her mother must have been when Daddy left her. "A charming man," her grandmother said. Yes, Daddy was a charming man, but thoughtless and self-centered as a child, as Jackie. But he wasn't supposed to be a little kid like Jackie. He was supposed to be grown up, and grownups were responsible—the way her mother was always responsible.

"I'm going to see where Jackie's gotten to," Chris said. She kissed her grandmother's cheek for no reason. "See you later, Mabel."

"Don't take any wooden nickels," Mabel called.

Jackie was standing on the bridge over the pond, staring at the water. Chris ran across the dewy lawn to join her. "Let's go for a walk in the woods and see if there are any ripe raspberries," Chris said.

"I don't feel like it."

"You going to go around acting gloomy for the rest of your life?"

"I don't care."

"Look, Jackie, it hurt me as much as you, maybe even more—what happened Saturday."

"You mean my rabbits?"

"Is that what you're all upset about? Just the rabbits?"

"No."

"What then?"

"I lost Grandma's silver coach."

"*What?* How did you do that? What did you do with it?"

"I took it down to the island to see if I could make the magic bring back my rabbits, and it fell off the bridge."

"Jackie!"

"Don't be mad at me, Chris. I couldn't help it. It just jumped out of my hand." Jackie's tears slipped down her cheeks and splashed on the log railing. Chris gave her a tissue from her pocket and hugged her.

"Stop crying and maybe we can figure out how to fish it up."

"How? The water's too dark and it's all weeds."

"We can try the fishing gear Mabel got us."

"You're not mad at me, Chrissie?" Jackie perked up.

"No. I'm sorry you lost it though. Come on. Let's see what we can do."

They tried the wooden shuttles wound with string, with hooks and sinkers attached, that Mabel had given them. Starting together in the middle of the bridge where Jackie thought she had dropped the coach, they took small steps away from each other toward opposite sides of the bridge, dropping the hooks in each time they moved, pulling them up, rewinding, and dropping them again.

Mabel, who was leaving, called to them across the lawn, "Hope you catch something, girls."

Chris waved at her and called goodbye. Jackie said to Chris, "We're never going to hook it."

"We'll try using a rake or maybe a long stick with a net at the end of it."

"A net would be good."

"Let's go see what we can find. I think I saw a butterfly net in the attic."

"Oh, Chris, you're so smart!"

"You're the one who's smart, Jackie."

"Only in school. At home you're the smartest."

The butterfly net had a few tears in it which Chris mended quickly.

"Going to start a butterfly collection?" Grandmother asked when Chris asked for permission to use it.

"We're fishing for something down at the pond," Chris said, carefully vague.

Grandmother nodded and went back to cleaning her refrigerator out. She always seemed to know when not to ask a lot of questions.

The rake was too short. Chris lay on her stomach on the muddy shore and reached the rake out as far as she could, dragging it through the weeds that grew in the water, first on one side of the bridge and then on the other. All she brought up was slimy grass and snails. Her clean T-shirt and jeans were coated with mud when she stood up.

"It's no use," Jackie said. "We'll never find it again."

"We'll find it," Chris said. "You know it's there, Jackie. We just have to keep trying."

Next Chris sent Jackie for some string. She wound the ends of the butterfly-net handle and the rake handle together and tried lying flat on the bridge and swishing the net at the end of the combined sticks slowly through the water as deep as it would go. When that did not work, she reversed her tool and tried holding the handle just below the wire net and letting the rake down into the water. The butterfly net had caught an orange carp nearly a foot long. The dumped it back along with dozens of tadpoles and a rusty can. The rake brought up only brownish weeds by the prongful, roots and all. All of a sudden Jackie screamed.

"I saw it!"

"Where?"

"It fell down when you pulled up the rake—there." She pointed, eyes and finger riveted to the spot like a setter pointing a bird. Carefully, Chris lowered the rake, wriggled it gently, and drew it up once, twice, three times. She changed her position slightly and tried again, once, twice, three times. She tried again a little farther out, stretching as far over the edge as she dared.

"I'm getting tired, Jackie. Maybe we should try again later."

Jackie held her point. Her mouth trembled with disappointment.

"Just twice more, then I have to stop for a while," Chris said, seeing her sister's face. She lowered the rake directly down and pulled it up hand over hand. It was dripping water and mud and grass. The half-buried carcass of the silver coach was caught in its claw.

Jackie squealed and grabbed the coach, mud and all. Chris lay down on her back in the sun, feeling peaceful and achey, while Jackie hurried down to the edge of the pond to wash off the coach, chattering all the while. "You're so great, Chrissie. You're so fantastic. The coach isn't hurt at all. I didn't think you'd ever find it, and Grandma would be so mad at me, and I—Oh, thank you!" She sat down next to Chris's slender body and kissed her nose. "I love you, Chrissie. You're the best sister."

Chris felt content. Impulsively she said, "Jackie,

would you like to fly somewhere with me in the silver coach?''

"Can you make it go for me?"

"Maybe."

"What do I have to do?"

Chris didn't feel like moving at all. The sun was kneading her with warm fingers, taking away the clamminess of her muddy clothes and leaving her sleepy and relaxed. "Lie down beside me and close your eyes," Chris said.

Obediently, Jackie lay down on the bridge. Her silky hair tickled Chris's chin.

"Now put your fingers on the coach. Touch the roof and think real hard about where you want to go," Chris said, and then, anxiously, "Do you feel a tingle?"

"Uh huh," Jackie reassured her.

"Good. Next everything will begin to ripple, like when you drop a stone in a pond, and the coach will get big and when you get in, the white horses will appear and then—"

"Will you come with me?" Jackie asked fearfully.

Chris smiled. "Sure I'll come with you. Take my hand. Close your eyes and wait." She didn't have to ask where Jackie wanted to go. For days now, homesickness had been growing in Chris alongside the hurt. If she was homesick, Jackie would be too. The coach would take them home.

For a while Chris thought nothing was going to happen this time. Then, quite suddenly, the shimmering began. The coach grew to full size, gleaming in the sunlight, as lovely as ever. Chris stepped in and helped Jackie to climb the high step. They sat side by side on the wire-lace seat. With no surprise, Chris noticed that her clothes were clean and dry. The horses appeared, their manes tossing like white wave crests, and the coach rose into the air. Chris put her arm protectively around Jackie's shoulder. The animals stretched their smooth necks out with the effort of flying. Their tails blew straight out behind them.

Below, the black macadam road wound through the green hills past dollhouse-sized farms and round-topped silos. They saw the Hudson River like a gray band separating the rows of houses, like mismatched boxes lining a pantry shelf, on either side of the river. Closer to home, when the coach flew lower, they could see their own street. A stickball game was going on.

Jackie's awed silence broke. "Hey everybody, look at us!" she shouted.

"No one can see us yet, Jackie," Chris explained. "The coach is invisible except when it's small, and the horses aren't real at all."

"Are we real?"

"Of course we're real."

As soon as they landed in their own driveway, Jackie jumped out. She ran up to the front door and rang the doorbell. Chris was right behind her when their mother, in her white nurse's uniform, opened the door.

"Jackie, Chris!" she cried with delight. "However did you get home? Oh, I'm so glad to see you."

She kissed and hugged them both at the same time while all of them laughed and cried and talked at once. They were home again. Their own familiar place took shape around them, fitting cozily. Their shared bedroom was just the same—messy on Jackie's side and neat on Chris's—with pictures of ballet dancers on the wall on Chris's side and pictures of animals on the wall on Jackie's side. The mobile with the stars hung down over their beds with the patchwork quilts their Grandmother Sissy had made for them. The stuffed animals used all the space in the chair in the corner. Jackie hugged all the animals she could fit in her arms and rolled on the beds with them.

"Tell me all about the summer," Mother said.

"Grandmother Wallace is a neat lady," Chris said. "She taught us how to do all kinds of things—bake and make preserves and make terrariums with tiny pine trees and lichen and stuff."

"And candles," Jackie said. "We made candles for you, Mommy."

Later, when they had set the table and their mother was making spaghetti and garlic bread, their favorites, for dinner, Chris said she would go outside to find her friends.

"Wait for me. I'm going to play stickball with everybody," Jackie said.

"Be back at five-thirty," Mother said, cheerfully smiling at them.

Chris found Seema and Amy sitting at the edge of Amy's pool. "Oh, Chris, you're home! We missed you," they said in unison, and it did not seem to Chris that they were shutting her out, rather that they were including her in a warm circle of three.

"Let's have a slumber party at my house tonight," Amy said. "I'll show you all the new things I learned in ballet class this summer. You'll have to practice a lot to catch up."

"But I will," Chris said. "I will catch up."

The sunshine was bright around their own neighborhood. The streets were filled with children and dogs and the coming and going of lots of people. Back at Grandmother's the house and trees seemed as dark and lonely as they had at the beginning of the summer. The mountains were too vast, and even Grandmother was not enough to fill the spaces.

That evening, when Grandmother was washing the dinner dishes and Chris and Jackie were drying, Grandmother said suddenly, "Are any of those rabbits out there yours, Jackie?"

Jackie couldn't see out the kitchen window over the sink, so she ran to the door with Chris right behind her. The yard was full of rabbits eating the clover that Grandmother did not like because it brought bees.

"Some of them look only half grown," Grandmother said. "They could be yours, Jackie."

"They *are* mine," Jackie said positively, though all Chris could see were humped backs and canoelike ears. Rabbits yes, but too alike to tell one from the other.

"I guess," Grandmother said, "you were such a good feeder that they grew up faster than we expected."

"They're doing just fine," Jackie said proudly. She sounded exactly like their mother.

12

Grandmother had grown so quiet that Chris thought something must be wrong with her. But Grandmother insisted she was fine and Chris didn't have much time to worry about it. Mother was coming on Saturday to take them home, and home was the place Chris yearned for most now. It didn't matter how busy they were making fancy, cooky-cutter tea sandwiches from loaves of white bread—so many Grandmother said she would have to have two parties with the leftovers, so many they filled the little space left in the freezer. It didn't matter how long they worked with lopping shears and scythes, cutting down weeds and tree limbs on the island, where Jackie had decided they should have a picnic lunch for Mother. No matter how packed their days were, the hours still dragged, slow as dripping water filling a can, slow as a flower unfolding.

But cans do fill and flowers finally open, and days sticky with anticipation do pass. On Friday Chris was packing the last of her belongings, collecting things of hers and Jackie's from all the unlikely corners to which they had somehow wandered. "Who left my sneakers in the watering can?" Chris asked irritably.

"Not me," Jackie said.

The sneakers remained an unsolved mystery. So did the fact that the suitcases they had come with would not hold all their belongings for the return trip, even though all that had been added was the new T-shirt and sandals Grandmother had bought for each of them. But most puzzling to Chris was Grandmother. Chris thought it might be the heat, or it could be that Grandmother was just worn out from having taken care of two young girls all summer, but certainly she was being unusually quiet.

"Are you feeling sick?" Chris asked.

"I'm fine."

"It's too hot to work. Let's sit down and have some lemonade now," Chris suggested, in case Grandmother was overtired.

"It is hot. I hope a breeze comes up tomorrow when your mother's here."

"It's funny," Chris said. "Jackie and I were so scared when we first came. You were a stranger then, but now—I'm so glad we got to know you."

"Me too," Grandmother said. But she didn't seem to want to talk about it. "Did you find all your books, Chris?"

"I think so."

All Friday, in fits and starts, Chris thought about her mother. Sometimes she thought way back to the happy times before the divorce began. She remembered how they used to sing together in the car, even on short errands. Jackie and she used to giggle helplessly when they tried to sing, "Row, row, row your boat . . ." in rounds and kept getting tangled and singing the same

94

words instead of each one keeping to her own part. Mother had a pretty voice. She sang "Down in the Valley" so beautifully that it made Chris's skin tingle. But then Chris would remember more recent times when Mother had been snappish and mean, and Chris would try to lie low to avoid the bite of her mother's misery. Suppose Mother was still being mean and Chris was still going to feel guilty and unloved—suppose nothing was changed when they got home!

To see if she had missed something in them, Chris got out all the letters her mother had written her, eight for the eight weeks they had been here. She and Grandmother and Jackie had each received one letter a week all to herself. Grandmother and Jackie had written back faithfully, but Chris had missed a week here and there. She did not think much of her mother's letters. Mostly they just asked questions about what Chris was doing or how she was getting along with Jackie and Grandmother, or she would comment on something Chris had written to her that Chris had already forgotten by the time Mother's letter arrived: "How nice that you saw the baby foxes in the woods" . . . "The best way to keep your skin from peeling is to rub some oil or cream in, and don't get too much sun at one time." Usually Mother's letter trailed off emptily. "Not much news from here. I spend all my time studying and trying to keep up with assignments. I'll be glad when the courses are over. Miss you, love, Mother." But even if they were dull letters, there *were* eight of them, one for each week. When Chris thought about it, she realized that the only time her mother could have fitted them into her tight schedule was late at night when she was very tired, before she went to bed. That had to mean more than just doing her duty; that had to mean caring a whole lot.

"You look lost in thought, Chris," Grandmother said.

"I was thinking."

"About what?"

"Nothing." Chris didn't want to say it out loud. Grandmother couldn't do anything about it anyway. Suppose Mother was still angry. "If Mother isn't any different—" Chris began, and ran out of words to match the shape of her worry.

"I suspect she'll be different," Grandmother said. "You're different."

"I am?"

"Definitely, and Jackie is too."

"How are we different?"

"Well, you're both more lovable."

"Jackie was always lovable," Chris said.

"Was she? When I first met you, you both had certain faults."

"What faults?" Chris was not at all surprised to hear that she had faults, but it amazed her that Jackie had them too.

"Let's see if your mother notices any changes in you," Grandmother said.

And what about Mother, Chris thought. Will she still yell at me for every little thing? Will it always be my fault? She remembered the day she had forgotten to make her bed, and Mother had made it, and Jackie had messed up the covers soon after, and Mother had screamed at Chris in front of her friends. If it was like that again, if it was like that . . .

Saturday morning time sat still as a rock in the sun. Chris felt loose nerve endings jumping under her skin. Grandmother was still maintaining her peculiar silence, and Jackie was skittering around aimlessly. It was still and hot outside. Just before noon Jackie said, "I can hear a car coming up the road.'' She dashed out the door.

Chris felt cold with anxiety as she put the paper cups into the picnic basket and started out the kitchen door, which Jackie had left wide open.

"The deviled eggs!" Chris cried, as if the picnic depended on them.

"I'll get them," Grandmother said. "You go greet your mother."

Chris looked at her grandmother. The clear, gray eyes were clouded with such sadness. Underneath the rapid beating of her heart, Chris wondered why her grandmother should be sad. But she had no time for wondering now. She bolted out the door screeching, "Mother!" just as the old green car with the rusted-out back fender pulled up alongside Jackie.

The furrow between her mother's eyes was deeper than ever, and her hair still lay in limp spaghetti strands around her head. Her eyes looked at Chris in a funny, questioning way as she bent and hugged and kissed Jackie.

"Hello, my darlings," Mother said in a husky voice. She reached out an arm to Chris, who kissed her.

"You look so tired," Chris said. "It must have been awful hard for you."

"It was," Mother said. "But I passed, and it's over now. You both look wonderful, you two. The summer here must have been good for you."

"Grandmother made it good," Chris said.

"Grandma knows how to do everything," Jackie said. "We're going to have a picnic on the island, Mommy, just for you."

"Lovely," Mother said, and she let them draw her into the house, where she greeted Grandmother and

97

gave her a present. "I hope you like it," Mother said. The present was a beautiful, heavy wool cardigan with pockets and bone buttons. "For the cool mornings and evenings," Mother said.

"Isn't it elegant!" Grandmother said and put it on immediately to model it for them, despite the heat. "How do I look, girls?" She rolled up the cuffs on her too-short arms and beamed at them all.

"You look ritzy, Grandmother," Chris said.

"Ritzy?" Mother questioned.

"That's Mabel's word. It means fancy," Chris said.

"Ritzy," Mother repeated. "I'll have to remember that."

"How was your trip?" Grandmother asked, taking off the sweater and folding it carefully.

"Long and hot, but I didn't care. I was so glad to be coming here. I missed you all." She smiled at Jackie. "How come you're so quiet, Jackie?"

"I'm listening."

"Are you *really*?" Mother laughed. "That's the first time I've ever known you to do that. How have you and Jackie been getting along, Chris?"

"Oh, fine," Chris said. "I think Jackie's maturing."

Grandmother and Mother glanced at each other, exchanging a smile as if Chris had said something amusing. She didn't know what. "Would you like some cold lemonade, Mother?" she asked.

First they showed their mother the bedspread tent. Mother enthused about it so much that Chris offered, "You can sleep here in my bed, and I'll sleep downstairs on the couch. It's cool enough up here at night, even though it feels hot now."

"No, my bed," Jackie said. "Mommy can have my bed, and I'll sleep on the couch."

"I feel like a special person," Mother said. "No-body's made so much fuss over me in—" She didn't say how long. A long, long time, Chris realized. She couldn't even remember a time when anyone fussed over their mother, not she or Jackie or their father, not even Grandma Sissy, who spent most of her time telling Mother what she was doing wrong with her house, her husband, her children, or herself. Grandma Sissy never complimented anyone, except sometimes herself.

The picnic on the island was a happy success. They spread a heavy rug over the stubble of weeds, and a sheet over that. A spongy carpet of moss made a damp backrest. Even the ants had plenty to eat, and a nuthatch kept circling the trunk of the tree nearby, watching them with one eye, head cocked as if he was just awaiting an invitation to join them.

"Delicious nutbread," Mother said, eating a second piece.

"Chris baked it," Grandmother said. "She's a naturally good cook, and she pitches in with the cleanup without being asked too. You did a fine job of bringing up your girls, Mary."

"I think I have to thank you for some of their bringing up," Mother said. "They've changed so much in these past weeks."

"How have we changed?" Chris asked, curious, looking at Grandmother, who smiled back as if to say, "I told you so."

"Well, Jackie's not demanding attention all the time, and you're—you're so thoughtful, so sweet."

"Me?" Chris asked unbelievingly. "Me, sweet?"

"Yes," Mother insisted. "You are sweet."

"Grandmother must be a witch after all then," Chris

said, pleased and then embarrassed in case she had hurt Grandmother's feelings.

"Grandma's our good white witch of Vermont," Jackie said, making it all right because they laughed. Chris was proud of Jackie for being so clever.

That evening they sat in the living room at the big table, watching the sun spread pink and purple above the mountains. Mother asked about places Grandmother had seen, and Grandmother talked about some of her experiences living in foreign countries. When Jackie dozed off in her chair, Grandmother woke her up and led her upstairs to bed, leaving Chris and her mother alone in the shadowy living room.

"Is Daddy going to marry that woman?" Chris asked.

Mother hesitated, then answered Chris as if they were friends instead of mother and daughter. "He told me he hopes to after the divorce is final. He says he's thinking of moving to California with her."

The answer was honest, but it jolted Chris. "California! I guess we won't see much of him then."

"Will you mind that?"

"I don't know," Chris said. "I think so." She and her mother looked at each other—really looked at each other like people who are going to have to get along together in close quarters for a long time—warily but with good will.

"You know what your grandmother wrote me?" Mother asked.

"What?"

"That if I gave you room to grow, I'd be surprised at what a special person you are . . . Did I nag you too much, Chris?"

"Sometimes you did. Sometimes I felt as if you

blamed everything on me and nothing I did was ever right.''

"Sometimes you didn't cooperate too much, you know.''

Chris nodded. "I know. I'm going to be nicer now.''

"I'm going to be nicer too," Mother said, and then her voice came low and soft, "Chris?''

"Yes?''

"I need you so much.''

"I need you too, Mother.'' Chris put her arms around her mother and they hugged each other. It made Chris cry to find her mother's cheeks were wet with tears.

Sunday morning the time that had moved so slowly yesterday slipped away faster than a falling raindrop. They rushed to pack the car and ran back after the fish that Jackie had found in the pond and insisted on bringing home in a gallon jar. Grandmother fed them all pancakes for breakfast and helped them carry everything out. She loaded all the leftover space in the car with fresh vegetables from the garden, but she was too quiet. Chris was disturbed that Grandmother had become so quiet.

"Grandma," Jackie said breathlessly, "I lost your silver coach, but Chrissie found it in the pond for me.''

"Oh really?" Grandmother laughed. She was wearing the new sweater in the dewy, cold morning. She reached into her pocket and pulled out the silver coach. It looked so fragile in her plump fingers. "Jackie," Grandmother said, "I hope you won't be mad at me, but I want to give this to Chris to keep. You may pick out something else you'd like to have as a keepsake from me, but the silver coach is Chris's.''

Jackie nodded, but Chris said, "Oh no, Grandmother! I couldn't take your coach.'' And looking at her grand-

101

mother's tear-filled eyes she understood the quietness that had come upon her. Grandmother was going to be lonely without them. "I want you to keep the coach," Chris said.

"Why, Chris?"

"Because you need it more than me. How else are you going to come see us if you don't have the silver coach?"

"Well, I could come in my old pickup truck, couldn't I?"

"You will come, won't you?" Mother said.

"You have to come and stay with us often," Chris said. "We're going to miss you awfully."

"Not as much as I'll miss you." Grandmother sniffed and hid her eyes behind a tissue as tears overflowed down her cheeks. "You sure you don't want to take the coach, Chris?" she asked when she had control of herself again.

"Pretty sure. If I change my mind, I'll write you," Chris said.

"Can you come to visit us tomorrow?" Jackie asked from her place in the front seat, snuggled next to her mother.

"Not quite that soon," Grandmother laughed.

"Thank you, Grandmother," Chris said.

"For what, darling?" Grandmother asked as Chris kissed her and got into the front seat next to Jackie.

"For all the magic," Chris said.

As the car pulled away, Chris watched her grandmother standing there, waving goodbye with her face scrunched tight as a dried apple against the sun and the silver coach gleaming softly in her hand.

"Nothing's ever the way you want it all the time," her grandmother had warned her this morning. Maybe she should have accepted the silver coach, Chris thought. Maybe she would need it. Probably she would sometimes, but, even so, she felt pretty sure, hopeful really, that it was going to be all right.